LAST CHANCE

K.N. NGUYEN

www.dragonscript.net

Cover design by Brian Flores and Francis Nguyen.

Layouts by Francis Nguyen.

ISBN-13 978-1-949322-19-4

To Tou, Alicia, and Miko

Your help has allowed this story to

Sing to the world

I

THE TRUMPETING BLASTS of the horagai rang in the air amidst the light, celebratory beats of the shime daiko. The smaller drums gave a lively tempo for the conch shells to declare the ship's victory. Cries from the deck echoed in the air, slowly changing into a song. Katō Akio wove through his shipmates as they danced and sang. Barrels of beer and sake flowed freely, mugs clanking and the spirits sloshing onto the deck. A flagon was shoved into Akio's hand, spilling beer down his front.

"Drink up, Katō!" Yamamoto Taka goaded. "If my guess is right, we're on the right path. Ryū-ō is said to leave his palace in the summer and enjoy the warm waters. Tonight we celebrate, for tomorrow we continue the hunt!"

With a mighty yell, Taka downed the remaining liquid in his mug, slapping Akio on the back as he wiped his mouth with his other hand.

"Tomorrow we hunt." The words came out softly from Akio's mouth as he watched Taka stagger away. No doubt the man had been celebrating since sun up when the first note of the horagai was blown.

This would be Akio's first hunt. He'd only joined the crew on the *Taihō* a few weeks back, but it already felt like home. He'd acclimated to a life at sea surprisingly quickly. But what made his new life on the *Taihō* so exciting was the promise of adventure and a new beginning.

Akio scanned the ship. Men and women played the taiko, the medium-sized chū daiko adding another layer to the higher pitched shime daiko and horagai. A few men brought out their shakuhachi, the bamboo flutes trilling over it all.

His time aboard the *Taihō* passed in a blur, completely overshadowed by the taiko. The drums intrigued him. When had history ever written about a group of sailors reveling with such an array of musical instruments like this? Upon boarding the ship, Akio promptly busied himself with finding out who led the drummers, hoping to be asked to join their group. Taka wasted no time in welcoming Akio and inviting him to observe their daily practice. Soon, he hoped to join their ranks. Every time Akio saw them playing, he remembered the countless hours spent practicing the piano. At least now he could play something that made him happy.

He continued to weave through the crew, flagon in hand. Several men attempted to push full mugs into his hand, but Akio turned them all away, motioning to the half-consumed drink already with him. It never seemed to matter. Cries of "more" were followed by laughter as they staggered away. In the back of his mind, a dim memory struggled to surface. Familiar shouts egging him on to continue drinking fought to break through to the forefront of his mind.

Akio found himself bobbing to the beat, a grin on his face. He couldn't think of a better way to live than to play music under the warm sun, the tangy sea air blowing in his face. Turning away from yet another proffered drink, he spied Inoue Saori sitting off to the side near the sake barrels. Her absence from the festivities made her stick out from the rest. Ignoring the calls of Taka to join him and a few others on the chū, Akio found himself drawn to Saori.

"Why aren't you celebrating?"

Saori's husky voice was different from the other women – sweet and dripping like honey. The question caught him off guard. Here she sat isolated, yet she probed him, calling him out for being different. It reminded him of how his sister used to chide him.

"I could ask you the same question." The words felt childish the moment they left his mouth. Sliding onto the deck,

Akio pulled his knees close to his chest. "Why aren't you out there?"

With a sigh, Saori tucked a sheet of hair behind her ear. Thick lashes rimmed her dark eyes. They shone with a fierce intelligence that Akio had rarely seen. He found himself wanting to wrap his arm around her, but he was certain she'd slap him away.

"After a while you lose the hope of ever seeing Ryū-ō."

Her voice came out heavy as if she'd given up hope long ago. In the background, men continued to dance and sing. The song of victory filled the air, traveling for miles in all directions for Man and gods to hear. Sudden booms, their deafening explosions shaking the *Taihō* and sending out waves from the blasts, heralded fireworks. Though the sun still hung in the sky, the vibrant colors didn't disappear in the lights. It was all so beautiful. Akio had never seen such a celebration before and couldn't stop the excitement and hope that swelled in his chest. Yet here Saori sat, her head down and gaze despondent.

When he first boarded, Yamada Mizuki gave him some advice about his new life on the *Taihō* – what to expect about his new duties and some words about the difficulties of leaving his old life behind. Before they stepped onto the ship, she mentioned Ryū-ō, the Dragon King. Akio had tried to remember something about the deity, but nothing came to mind about the sea god and master of serpents. Her words about how he was responsible for the tides, representing both the perils and bounty of the sea filled him with wonder. He imagined the majestic god and his magic jewels guiding ships through raging storms. When she told him that he also granted those he deemed worthy a wish, Akio nearly exploded with childish joy. Akio vowed then and there to find the dragon and earn his gift.

"There is always hope," he said, grabbing her hand and giving it a squeeze. "Yamamoto and the others wouldn't be so sure if there wasn't." He wanted to believe it, anyway. It felt a little hypocritical for him to say that given his past, but at this moment, Akio truly believed it.

Saori met his gaze. A small smile crept across her face, but Akio couldn't help but wonder if it was a look of pity. Returning his gesture, she motioned for him to get up.

"You sound like I did when I first joined *Taihō*." Her tone bit him, the sudden shift from tenderness catching him off-guard. Once more, her tone changed, the whiplash startling Akio. "I guess it doesn't hurt to keep believing."

"Yamamoto told me that Ryū-ō is full of surprises. Who knows? This could be our chance to see an actual god!" Akio's voice quivered with excitement as he spoke. Every emotion he'd felt when he first boarded the *Taihō* came flooding back to him. "How long have you been searching?"

Taka never told him how long the *Taihō* and her crew had been chasing after the mighty sea dragon. Based on the weathering of the ship's wood and how sun-kissed their skin was, it couldn't have been long.

"At least thirty years," Saori replied. Her voice dropped as though she were preventing it from cracking. "You lose track after a while."

Akio's jaw dropped. Saori didn't look much older than his sister. Her hair shone with a dazzling luster; her face was perfection without a blemish or a wrinkle. How could she have been searching for an elusive god for thirty years?

"Were you a child?" he began.

"Look!" she exclaimed, popping up as she pointed out on the deck.

Akio's head snapped in the direction she indicated, all thought of their conversation forgotten. In the distance, Taka and some of the others stepped up to the taiko and began playing a powerful song. The beats were earnest but strong. Those who played on the shime daiko kept this new song steady, unwavering as those on the chū beat their entreaty to the mighty god. Then came the rumbling from the largest drum – the ōdaiko. A slim woman with short hair played the drum, each strike against its head sending a beat that resonated deep within Akio's body.

"Yamada-sama," Saori whispered. "She's beginning the hunt early."

Akio turned to Saori, trying to sputter out a question, but she held up a hand to silence him. A new light shone in her eyes, sparkling fiercely. Hope had been rekindled within her.

"Who is she?" he asked softly, awe seeping into his voice. "She must be important. She brought me here. But I've never seen her at practice with Yamamoto or the others."

"You wouldn't," Saori replied with a shake of her head. "Apart from the captain, there's no one higher than her. She's been here longer than me. I think only Matsumoto-sama has been here longer. They're really close, like father and daughter."

The pair stood quietly as Mizuki's strikes picked up in tempo. Her petite figure belied the strength within.

"If she is heading the call for Ryū-ō, it must be true." Saori's eyes twinkled with hope. "We must be close this time. It's been years since he was last seen."

Her enthusiasm intrigued Akio. He struggled with asking her about what happened when they found the dragon god of the sea. Had she been disappointed too many times? Was Ryū-ō that elusive? The prospect of finding the great beast set his heart racing.

"What happens once we catch Ryū-ō?" Akio had to raise his voice to almost a yell to be heard over the music and the explosions from the fireworks.

"No one knows. The wish is only granted to one person at a time. I've never figured out how they get chosen." Grabbing Akio's hand, Saori yanked him to his feet. Her hair fanned out as she spun to face him. "Come! If we don't join in, the elders warn it is bad luck. Besides, you still need to get used to playing with everyone. The music can change and you need to be able to adjust or you'll get lost."

Leaving Akio behind, Saori took off to join a group of people handing out chappa. The hand cymbals added a bright tone to the music in between the fireworks explosions. Soon, she was dancing around the deck, a dazzling smile illuminating her face. Not wanting to miss out on the festivities, Akio made his way over to Taka, who promptly handed him a pair of thick drumsticks and led him over to a free drum.

The bachi felt slick in Akio's hands. Having never held drumsticks of any kind, Akio found the bachi slipping around in his palms. Worn down over the years from hand oils, the portion he held were darkening to brown. His first few strikes on the drum felt awkward and clumsy. His timing was off, his beats a half second behind the others.

"Relax and feel the song," Taka said, clapping Akio on the back. "We all start as beginners, but trust me, you'll pick it up in no time if you keep with it."

"How long until you felt comfortable?" Akio asked.

"Two or three years," Taka replied with a wink. As Akio gasped in confusion, Taka couldn't help but chuckle. "You didn't think we'd expect you to play at our level so quickly, did you?"

"Of course not," Akio said, his face warming as blood rushed to his cheeks. "The music is just so infectious and every is so talented. I thought I would be able to keep up better." Akio's cheeks burned as embarrassment overwhelmed him.

"Don't worry, Katō," Taka said, slapping his shoulder jovially. "You'll have plenty of time and I'm sure you'll pick it up fast."

The celebration carried on late into the evening. The drinks flowed freely, the songs of entreaty and praise to the great Ryū-ō rang into the night, echoing for miles in every direction, and the fireworks continued to dazzle the heavens with their splendid colors. Akio found himself lost in the music, his earlier hesitations about not being able to keep up with the rest of the crew having vanished long ago. Now, he played with passion, his own soul spilling out with each strike against the drum. The joy surrounding him was contagious.

On more than one occasion, Akio spied Saori performing on the other side of the deck. She alternated between playing the chappa and the ōdaiko. Whenever Saori would step up to the big drum, both she and Mizuki struck the drum with such force that Akio felt it in his bones. Their movements were identical having spent years together, each strike landing with precision. Their improvised sections flowed together like a fish swimming through the ocean's currents. The harmony inspired Akio to master the chū.

It wasn't until the early hours of the following morning that the ship began settling down to sleep. The drinking and singing died down, leaving only the beating of the taiko. Mizuki stood in front of the ōdaiko once more, her strong figure silhouetted in the pale light of the moon. The calm waters reminded Akio of glass. There wasn't even the slightest ripple. As Mizuki faced the large drum, all other instruments fell silent, save for the shime. Raising her voice to the heavens, Mizuki prayed for success and safe travels on their search for Ryū-ō. As her plea echoed in the still night, she struck the ōdaiko three times.

All was quiet aboard the *Taihō*. The celebration was over, and once the sun rose, the adventure began. Akio suddenly found himself exhausted and his body sore. Making his way down to the sleeping quarters inside the ship, Akio wondered what the next few days would bring. Saori said she'd been searching for thirty years. Curling up in his cot, Akio pondered if it would take another thirty. He fell asleep dreaming of the great dragon god and his adventures hunting for it.

II

EMPTY BEDS and the gentle rocking of the *Taihō* greeted Akio as he woke up. The drums and other instruments rested neatly in their spots, out of the way from anyone who may be passing by. The sound of general chatter and the clanking of pots or pans in another part of the ship suggested breakfast was being made. Akio's stomach rumbled in excitement. Usually, they ate whatever fish they caught, but the presence of more substantial cookware gave him hope that there'd be something more filling on special occasions.

Emerging into the bright sunlight, Akio saw a pot of miso burbling over the built-in hearth. As the cook stirred the soup, his ladle sifted through a bit of seaweed they must have brought onto the ship. Silver sea bass on skewers cooked over the fire. The sight of such a hearty meal made Akio's stomach rumble once more. Shielding his eyes from the sun, Akio realized he did not have a headache from yesterday's festivities.

While in school and during the early days of his career, Akio's friends and work colleges teased him about his inability to handle his liquor. The hangovers were brutal, knocking him out for hours if not longer. Today, he felt just fine. Akio struggled to remember the last time he'd drank so freely. Perhaps he had consumed too much because Akio could not recall the last time he drank with friends or family. He just remembered the jokes people made about him whenever he would stumble around intoxicated. It was as though a door had shut on those memories, blocking their laughing faces from surfacing. Even their voices sounded muffled.

"Strange," Akio murmured as he rubbed his temple.

"What's strange?" Taka asked, bounding over to Akio as he stood rooted to the deck in confusion.

"I thought I would feel horrible after yesterday."

Taka slapped Akio on the back with a laugh. "I remember how much we celebrated my first hunt. The alcohol must not be as strong because I wasn't even fazed. I should've been stumbling around, I had so much. Maybe they are truly spirits blessed by the gods because I've never seen anyone suffer from too much drink."

Scanning everyone on the deck, Akio noted how no one appeared to be nursing a hangover. General chatter punctuated the otherwise peaceful morning. No one appeared pale or ill. No one seemed bothered by the particularly brilliant light that morning or the glare from the sails. Even in the sleeping quarters there wasn't anyone sleeping in or buried under their blanket, protecting their eyes from the sun. It made sense for the alcohol to not be very strong. A ship full of wasted sailors was probably not the best idea – people might slip overboard. The scent of miso caught Akio's attention once more, making his mouth water. Shaking away his concerns, Akio turned towards the breakfast line.

"I told you, Katō. It's nice on the *Taihō*. Where else can you enjoy good company and unimagined adventure? Where else can you chase a literal god? There is no place I'd rather be than on this ship."

Taka's eyes sparkled as he spoke. Though he was older than Akio, Taka radiated a boyish energy as he spoke. It was infectious, and Akio found himself smiling in return.

"Nowhere."

In the back of his mind, questions about the elusive dragon god and what types of wishes he granted swirled about. Somehow, they were also hidden behind doors, fighting for his attention. Instead, Akio let them fade. He would ask them later. Right now he wanted food. And to settle into his routine now that they were beginning their hunt. There was still so much to learn and other questions waiting to be asked.

Taka nodded in approval, drawing Akio from his reverie, and motioned to follow him for food. Akio trailed behind ready to eat.

"You'll realize soon enough that life on the *Taihō* is absolute paradise."

"Hey Yamamoto," Akio asked as he picked up a silver bowl for food. "How long have you been on the *Taihō*?"

"Not long," Taka replied absentmindedly. "Most of us have been here maybe a few years."

A wistful look flitted across Taka's face. Akio's brow furrowed as Taka filled his bowl with miso and threw a few silver bass on top. That didn't seem right to Akio. Taka told him the day before that it took two to three years to feel comfortable playing the taiko, and he was one of the best on the ship. Could he just be naturally talented? After filling his own bowl, Akio wandered off after waving good-bye to Taka and the group he joined, despite their requests that he eat with them. Akio searched for a more secluded spot to eat his breakfast. The nagging questions he'd pushed away earlier were calling to him once more.

"How can it only have been a few years?" Akio muttered as he pushed his spoon through the soup. "It doesn't make sense. He's one of the higher ups. Is he like Yamada-sama?"

The thought gave Akio pause. How long had Mizuki been aboard the *Taihō*? If Saori had been here around thirty years and Mizuki longer, it stood to reason that Taka had at least thirty years under his belt on the ship. He was so well respected and such a phenomenal player, he even greeted Akio and took him under his wing when Akio first arrived. Taka's big brother persona matched the notion that he would only be sailing for a few years, but something tickled the back of Akio's mind. Saori didn't look older than the local high schoolers by his home. What if Taka didn't age either? Akio chased the thought away. It was ridiculous to think that they wouldn't age. But why would Taka lie? There was nothing to gain by saying he'd been here for a shorter period of time.

The soup cooled down to a disappointing lukewarm temperature by the time Akio took his first sip. So did the fish. Choosing to eat in silence, Akio watched the inhabitants of the *Taihō* as they began their morning routine. Everyone moved with a spirited step, calling out to each other about what they would do once they encountered the mighty Ryū-ō. They worked with an efficiency that confirmed that they weren't new to the ocean life, but the way they spoke led Akio to believe that they didn't know much.

"I don't understand," Akio said softly to himself.

"What don't you understand?" Saori's question cause Akio to jump, nearly spilling his mostly uneaten soup onto his lap.

"Oh shit!" he gasped. "Don't do that again."

"Sorry," she replied sheepishly, tucking a loose strand of hair behind her ear. A smirk played on her lips, as she fought back the grin. "What are you doing here by yourself? I thought you'd be preparing to find Ryū-ō with Yamamoto and the others. Senchou will be speaking soon."

Blinking, Akio debated on whether or not he wanted to open up to Saori. Questions still swirled around in his head, and while he didn't necessarily mistrust her, everything left him feeling confused. Too many things were unanswered, unexplained. Why couldn't he keep the awe and excitement he first felt when he boarded the *Taihō* three weeks ago? It was all so simple back then.

A small surge of indignation seeped, muddying his emotions. How dare his carefree life suddenly become so baffling. Akio had told himself that after the long hours working, his reward was to finally find a bit of freedom from all of life's responsibilities. The competing sentiments twisted his stomach uncomfortably.

"You were alone yesterday," he replied, willfully pushing away his discomfort. He chose to ignore it all, instead welcoming the excitement with open arms. "Is it so unusual to find people needing a moment to themselves?" Immediately he regretted his word choice. Despite his internal turmoil, they were far too harsh for what he meant to say.

"You're right." The sudden drop in tone created a pit in Akio's stomach. "We all need alone time."

"That's not what I meant," Akio said hurriedly as Saori's gaze dropped. He thought he saw tears catch in her lashes. "I just meant – "

"You meant that you want to be alone," she said. "I get it."

Shoving herself off the ground, Saori briskly walked off, leaving Akio sputtering an apology mixed in with his cry of confusion. The clatter of his spoon falling to the ground reverberated in the strangely muted silence. Men moved about, continuing their morning routine as if nothing happened. No one acknowledged the conversation between Akio and Saori. It left him feeling strangely isolated on the ship despite him being close to most aboard.

Food no longer interested Akio, and he placed his bowl on the deck with a sigh. The soup was basically untouched and only the bass' scales were scraped due to him playing with his meal. Knowing he'd regret it in a few hours, Akio returned his food to the scrap bucket to be cleaned before heading to the sleeping quarters to begin his chores.

Being the newest member of the *Taihō*'s crew, Akio's duties started off relatively light – making the beds and cleaning the taiko and other instruments. Setting to work, Akio folded all the blankets, placing them on a shelf in the corner of the room. Next, he swept and dusted the entire room, taking special care to tend to the taiko and bachi. Previous conversations with various crew members let him know that the drums were more than just ceremonial or for celebrations.

"You'll find out soon enough," he'd been told with a knowing expression.

The words echoed ominously in the background of his mind as he tried to solve the morning's puzzle. Could they be related? Akio never excelled in music or history in school, but he had a basic understanding of taiko and the significance of ensemble drumming in the modern era. Wiping between the ring handles of the drum, Akio tried to put the morning's conversations with Taka and Saori out of his mind. He had enough with his own questions to keep him occupied. Turning the kan felt like turning the page of a book.

"Clearly I had too much to drink," Akio told himself. "There's no other way to explain it."

"Explain what?"

The deep bass of whoever stood behind him startled Akio, causing him to jump as the kan slapped against the side of the drum with an agonizingly loud smack. Did everyone on this ship move like cats? Spinning to face the stranger, Akio found himself face to face with an elderly man. His snowy, short-cropped hair looked almost grey against his weathered skin. Unlike most aboard, he seemed to be the oldest soul on the

Taihō. Deep wrinkles lined his face, especially around his eyes and mouth. Akio hoped that meant he was a jovial man.

A small insignia on the collar of the elderly man's shirt caught Akio's attention. A beam of light landed on the sigil, making the thread shine. Staring back at him was a small fox. An orange glow almost appeared to engulf the elderly man like a halo.

"Matsumoto Toshio, captain of the *Taihō*," the man prompted when Akio offered no response.

Akio stopped staring at the fox, his attention snapping to the elderly man facing him. Remembering that he'd been asked a question, Akio's mind raced to recall it.

"N-nothing Senchou," Akio wished his voice didn't tremble like that. There was no indication he'd done anything wrong – except ignore the captain, and drop the kan – and already his voice betrayed him. "I was just wondering how everyone is so skilled with the taiko after being on the *Taihō* for just a few years. When I learned piano it took me ages, and I was still terrible."

A smile crossed Toshio's face, deepening his wrinkles and giving him a grandfatherly appearance. The fox caught another beam of light and twinkled. Akio's body relaxed a little, his breath still caught in his throat as he waited for the captain's response.

"My boy, our talents take time to grow – both in life and on the *Taihō*. Don't lose your faith. All that is worth doing is worth waiting for."

Warmth flooded Akio. The captain reminded him of his own grandfather who passed away when he was ten. The two had a special bond despite it being so short lived. A faint memory pushed its way to the surface of his mind. Thousands of orange torii leading to the Fushimi Inari shrine. His grandfather had insisted in visiting the Shinto temple during one of their visits to Kyoto when Akio was small. His grandfather, though Buddhist, had been fascinated with the various shrines and tried to visit a few each year.

"Harmony leads to transcendence," he once said. "Sometimes we need to remember the past to protect our future."

A wave of emotions rushed over Akio, his eyes prickling as tears threatened to spill out. It had been a long time since he'd heard his grandfather's voice. Toshio must have noticed the cloud that passed over Akio because he motioned for Akio to sit on the shelf holding the sheets next to him.

"How is your time on the *Taihō*?" Toshio's voice took on a softer quality. Akio confirmed that he must be a grandfather by the way he spoke.

"It's been wonderful. Everything is surreal, especially since everyone is so nice. It's almost like a dream. I can't believe it's all real."

It was now time for a cloud to darken the captain's countenance. The emotions swirling within him seeped through his grandfatherly veneer. To his credit, Toshio masked it well considering how much must have been roiling underneath.

"Do you miss your past life?" Toshio asked.

Akio paused, his face scrunching in concentration as he became lost in thought. "You know," he said slowly, his voice rising as though he asked a question. He remembered the doors, and how everything seemed shut behind them. "I don't remember too much. It... it all blurs together. I'm getting a feeling of some emotions, but I can't recall anything specific. Maybe it's the alcohol?" His ears burned in shame as he admitted to his overindulgence.

Toshio wrapped his arm around Akio's shoulders, squeezing them lightly. The affectionate expression returned, all traces of whatever troubled him earlier erased. Akio found himself leaning into the captain's embrace. The warmth felt just like his own grandfather's.

"Why can't I get clear memories?" Akio asked." I remember my grandfather, but nothing specific."

"Your time on the *Taihō* will make the past seem like a distant memory, I'm afraid. This new chapter will help you move forward. Hopefully, the memories won't fade. That -" Toshio's gaze dropped once more. "That is the hardest challenge most on here face. Time will answer most questions."

Placing his palms on his knees, Toshio pushed himself up with a grunt. "After all this time, it doesn't get easier," he said with a wink. "I'll see you on deck shortly. There's much to discuss about this hunt. And of course, you deserve your official welcome. It's the highlight, after all."

Toshio shuffled out of the sleeping quarters, leaving Akio alone on the shelf. The dusty rag lay forgotten on the floor by the taiko he'd been cleaning earlier. Leaning back against the wall of the ship, Akio closed his eyes and let himself reminisce. Small flashes of memories came to him – holding hands with his mom and dad, eating ice cream with his little sister, a big hug from his mother as he lay sick in bed. All of it came fast, and every time he tried to hold onto it, the scene faded to black. He tried recalling something more recent. His girlfriend Yumi's smile would light up a room, but try as he might, it would not come to him. A tear rolled down his cheek. How had he lost so much? Damn sake.

"I'll never drink again," he swore, picking up the rag to continue his dusting.

The rest of his work was completed in frustrated silence. His hands did not move the instruments as delicately as before. Instead of gentle rubbing, Akio wiped the cloth over the smooth wood almost haphazardly. Once finished, Akio threw the soiled rag into a basket filled with other pieces of laundry waiting to be washed.

Outside, a general rumbling of conversation let him know Toshio's speech had not started yet, but probably would shortly. Making his way to the deck, Akio ignored several greetings called out to him. Normally, he would look for Taka or one of the others he felt close to. This time Akio squeezed his way through the crowd, opting to stand next to the side of the ship, his elbow resting on the ledge, in silence. From the corner of his eye, he spied Saori. She always appeared to be alone as well. With a heavy blink, Akio forced himself to look away from her.

The last of the stragglers made their way onto the deck, joining the crew. Chatter continued with occasional spikes in volume. Sweat beaded on Akio's brow as the sun beat down on him. Many men onboard were shirtless for this reason. Gulls cawed overhead, their cries sounding over the whip of the sail as a gust of wind filled it. Finally, the noise died down as Mizuki positioned herself behind the ship's wheel at the helm. Akio had only been on the *Taihō* for three weeks, but he was starting to learn the crew and their ranks. Being one of the few women onboard, Mizuki remained an enigma, usually choosing to remain below deck.

"My friends," Mizuki called out.

Her mousy voice surprised Akio. He expected one filled with power to match the strong figure he'd seen the day before.

"Before our Honorable Captain addresses us, I wanted to offer a warm welcome to our newest member." Motioning towards Akio, how she found him so easily in the throng he couldn't even guess, she continued. "Katō Akio joins us at an amazing time – before we begin our journey for the great Ryū-ō." Cheers broke out from the crowd. "I have been reviewing everyone's birth dates and the elements, and it has shown me that we are close. Luck shines on the *Taihō*!"

More cheers rang out, too loud for Mizuki to even try and say anything else. The swelling of emotion was infectious and Akio found his sour mood disappearing as he let out an involuntary cry of joy with the others. He didn't know why he cheered, but his chest swelled with hope. He would find his answers – maybe even from Ryū-ō.

The euphoria built until it reached a peak and died down. Inside Akio, emotions continued to swirl around, searching for release. The quietness left him feeling unsatisfied. However, it was soon apparent why everyone else went silent. Toshio had arrived.

Unlike his time with Akio in the sleeping quarters, the captain carried an imposing air as he stood before his crew. He stood tall. Proud. Strong. All traces of the grandfatherly figure lay hidden behind his power. There was no vulnerability to be found.

"Thank you for your warm welcome," Toshio said to the now mute group. "I am always touched by your kindness. Today is a glorious day, and I know that together we will be successful. As you know, I have been on the *Taihō* a long time, but for our newest member to our family, allow me a moment for background. Though she doesn't look like it, the *Taihō* is an old ship." Patting the wheel fondly, Toshio continued.

"But she is powerful. She has led our search for Ryū-ō for countless generations, and through it all, we have supported each other as family. Now, the question I have been asked more times than I can count: Why do we chase? My friends, we do so for honor. We pursue the great sea dragon to receive his gift. What is it? Only the one who is chosen will know. It is a mystery to the rest of us, one that fuels our desire and eagerness to hunt."

The captain fingered the mon on his shirt, a flash of sunlight catching the little fox sigil embroidered on the fabric. The threads were so vibrant. Akio found himself leaning forward, drinking in Toshio's every work. Akio hadn't been told all of this when he first arrived on the *Taihō*, and knowing that there was some divine reward for one lucky individual made his mind run wild with ideas.

"But we also chase," Toshio continued, "to offer our protection to Ryū-ō. We are his guardians from those who wish to harm him, those who do not understand his purpose. In return, we are blessed with his gift."

"Who would want to hunt a god?" Akio muttered.

As if he heard Akio's question, Toshio said, "Those who do not know Ryū-ō's true form, the foreigners and superstitious seafarers who go after him for sport or glory, they pose the biggest threat to the mighty dragon. It is our duty to protect him at all costs. It is through Ryū-ō that we are able to continue our journey on these very waters, despite our eternal quest for redemption. Through Ryū-ō, we will find transcendence."

The intensity of the captain's speech pushed all other thoughts from Akio's mind. A desire to find the sea dragon god and both protect the mighty beast as well as vie for a chance to receive his holy gift blazed within him. At that moment, Akio swore that he would do whatever it took to achieve both goals.

"And so," Toshio concluded, "I welcome you all once more to the *Taihō* family. Now, to honor and glory!"

Toshio pumped his fist into the air. Every soul on deck followed suit, breaking out into a victorious cheer that drowned out all sound nearby. Akio joined in, the fevered energy making him want to run or jump - something to physically release what had built within. He scanned the deck, landing on Taka and a small group returning from below deck with a glass of sake. When had they snuck off to grab it? A tap on the shoulder distracted Akio as the man next to him offered a glass of sake. Akio saw someone pouring out glasses and passing them around.

Downing the contents, Akio felt the urge to pick up a pair of bachi and beat out a song. The energy was reminiscent of the day before. A few cries punctuated the revelry before a peppy tune burst forth from a pair of shime. Akio left his spot in search for a pair of bachi. He managed to locate a pair, making his way to Taka and the others on the chū daiko. The first strike felt different from yesterday. He felt confident, more sure of himself. As Akio and the other chū daiko players expressed their joy through music and dance, Akio found himself feeling lighter than he had in a long time.

His arms moved in time with the others, a smile plastered on his face the entire time. Ōkedō players, the drums hanging from red silk straps with golden embroidery around their shoulders, joined in. Those with ōkedō danced around on deck. Akio didn't remember seeing anyone playing ōkedō during yesterday's festivities, but the faint glimmer of a childhood memory where he saw a taiko performance during some special event flickered in the back of his mind. It was promptly forgotten when he noticed a sheet of dark hair disappear into the depths of the ship.

Akio turned back to his chū, letting the music carry him away. The deep resonating booms of Mizuki playing the ōdaiko accented the song. She didn't add to the back beat or flourish it with her own touch. Instead, she struck select beats that accented the other drums. The ship lurched to the side as Toshio turned the ship's wheel. The *Taihō* headed towards the endless deep blue. Their journey had begun.

III

THE SUN BEAT DOWN on the *Taihō*, heating the deck and soaking her crew in sweat. Akio's shirt stuck to his flesh, his hair matting on his head as he sat in the scant shade above deck. Swirling his mug, Akio took a final drink of water before shoving the empty cup away. Mizuki stood at the helm overseeing the crew on deck with her hands behind her back. Time passed without any sight of land or the mighty sea dragon. Vast blue water as far as the eye could see, that was the only landscape Akio could watch these many days. Only the placement of the stars provided any indication of their movement. If only he could track them.

In the weeks that had passed after Toshio's speech regarding the hunt, Akio found he was no closer to getting any answers than he'd been after his first conversation with Saori. No one knew when Ryū-ō appeared or how he chose someone for a gift. He also tried to find out how long people had been on the ship or about their lives before the *Taihō*. Whenever he got to these questions, there would be a pause, and the conversation would change. Whoever he asked wouldn't be upset. As a matter of fact, they seemed unsure. However, a couple quickly ended the conversation with a concerned expression as though they were trying to answer some questions of their own. Later the same day, they'd be back to their usual selves. Either they were putting on an act or they found closure. Their nonchalance unnerved Akio for some reason.

After the excitement of the moment dissipated, Akio wondered if he had heard the captain's speech before. He realized it was the same speech he'd heard when he first arrived on the ship. This brought him more questions. No one seemed to notice that the same message was being used over and over. Just another question for him to answer.

An excited cry from the starboard side brought a handful of men to the side of the ship. Intrigued, Akio sauntered over hoping it would be worth giving up his spot in the shade. A smattering of chatter from the crew and pointing greeted Akio as he walked up.

"It's a good sign!" Watanabe exclaimed. Akio made a mental note to find out the man's full name. "I've heard the fishermen talk about how rare they are."

"What is it?" Oda asked.

"One of the giant squids. It might even be a colossal squid." Watanabe's voice trembled in excitement as he rushed to get his words out. "Both live deep below the surface. Something must have driven it up. Maybe it was Ryū-ō."

Gasps of wonder and awe broke out from the group. Akio glanced down at the enormous creature. A large dish-sized eye gazed up at him. He didn't believe the animal was particularly intelligent, but he thought he saw a flicker of something flash through as they locked eyes. Behind him, men talked about the squid, joking about what a feast they could have. As calls for a net rang out, Akio found himself heading back to his little patch of shade.

Thoughts of what lay beneath the surface in those infinite depths swirled around his mind. How deep down could the sea dragon go? He's a god, so naturally there must be unbelievable strength to him. He is a dragon *and* a god. On several occasions, the crew talked about his palace and the splendor of his immortal riches. Akio wondered if Ryū-ō's palace was like the emperor's and if there were others in Ryū-ō's court.

Closing his eyes and leaning back against a barrel, Akio listened to the gulls cry overhead and the snap of the sail's fabric as it caught a gust of wind. The breeze cooled his matted hair, providing him with a small respite from the heat.

Akio wondered what he'd done that blessed him with the opportunity to chase a god. To possibly even receive a divine blessing. He'd never been particularly religious growing up, only going to the temple for his mother and grandparents' sake. He barely knew the gods' names.

Seeing as his new life was on the water, Akio wondered if the Shinto water god Suijin existed, and if so, was there a possibility the god would show himself? If Ryū-ō could be found, it wasn't too far-fetched to think that they might run into Suijin or another god. Buddhist or Shinto, a god was a god, right? His thoughts about Shintoism and Buddhism began to spiral as he questioned their legitimacy. Pushing his reservations aside, Akio admitted to himself that he was probably the worst person to go down this line of thinking. His knowledge of either religion was woefully inadequate and he was never one to engage in philosophical debates. It felt like he was just going in circles and not even getting a fun thought experiment trying to figure it all out.

Instead, Akio recalled his grandfather's funeral. Even as a little boy, he didn't want to wear the traditional white or sit through the service. The incense burned his nose, and he remembered his mother elbowing him as the priest chanted in the background. An intense sadness overwhelmed Akio. He hadn't thought of that day in a long time.

"Senchou really has me reminiscing," Akio mumbled, his eyes still closed.

Allowing his mind to wander once more, Akio found himself thinking about the men Toshio spoke about. Foreigners and seafarers. Superstitious men. He wondered if there might even be pirates. Were those people actually pirates? Was the crew of the *Taihō*? Could there even be good pirates? Childhood memories of watching cartoons with his little sister of treasure-hunting pirates brought a warm wave of nostalgia. His mother always snapped at the two to turn off the show and get to sleep as they huddled under a blanket in an effort to not be noticed as they watched.

"You look like you're having a serious conversation with yourself." The playful tone of the voice kept him from opening his eyes in confusion. There weren't many women aboard anyway.

"Are you still mad at me?" Akio finally cracked one eye open.

"I wasn't mad," Saori replied casually, slipping down to take a seat next to him. "Disappointed."

That hurt Akio more than if she'd said she had been mad. "I'm sorry," he muttered. "I had a lot on my mind that day, but I shouldn't have snapped at you."

Saori waved his apology away. Akio found himself wanting to wrap his arms around her shoulders. He missed the physical intimacy he'd had with his girlfriend and wanted to feel close to someone again.

"I see a lot of myself in you," she said, breaking the silence. "At least in the beginning. You're acclimating better though. And you have Yamamoto. He's good to keep nearby."

Akio thought he noted a hint of bitterness in her tone. Did she not like Taka or was she jealous? His stomach clenched and his arm trembled as he placed his right arm over her shoulders. When she didn't bat him away, he pulled her in towards him. Her soft sigh broke a small piece of him. Saori's hair brushed against his arm, sending a shiver down his spine. It also smelt of eucalyptus, the scent reminding him of his little sister, Miyako. Saori didn't easily rest against Akio. Instead, she sat stiffly letting him hold her.

"It bothers you that I have a – a group of friends?" Akio wondered if he would truly call the group his friends. Taka most likely, but the others he wasn't quite so sure. They all just congregated together, joking and sharing each other's company. "I noticed you speak so informally to everyone."

"It's not that," Saori replied glumly. "It's a little difficult to explain."

"Try me."

Akio met Saori's gaze, a half smirk on his face. He could see her studying his face, trying to see if he were serious. Giving her a small shake as he still held her, Akio let a goofy grin replace the half smirk.

"Oh fuck off," Saori said, the muscles on her face relaxing as she playfully slapped Akio's knee.

A hint of pride welled inside Akio. Every time he'd run into Saori, she was alone. He'd observed the melancholy written on her face, and the pain she must carry within by the way she moved. Today, he'd managed to make her happy. It turned out to be one of the best feelings he'd experienced on the *Taihō*. He wanted to see where the conversation would lead when a voice cried out from the crow's nest: "Unknown flag approaching! Starboard side!"

Akio and Saori's heads snapped to the right side of the *Taihō*. In the distance, the faint outline of an approaching ship could be seen. Mizuki and Toshio emerged from below deck, taking their spot at the helm. In Toshio's hand a spyglass pressed against his eye.

"Damn," the captain spat. "Any sign of whose flag?" he called out to the crow's nest.

It took an agonizing couple of minutes as more of the crew rushed to the deck before they received an answer.

"A raven."

"Shit," Saori muttered, pushing Akio's arm off her as she stood up.

"What is it?" Akio asked, scrambling up after her.

His heart raced as the people on deck began moving taiko into position. A few had strapped swords to their hips. The sudden sight of weapons made Akio's mouth run dry.

"Those damn Kingr," Saori explained. "Between them and the Zhōnghuá, the Kingr are more persistent. The Zhōnghuá, however, are more dangerous. Both are bad news."

More people spilled onto the deck from below, the taiko meticulously put into place. Akio stared at the drums dumfounded.

"Why the hell are we bringing these up?" Akio asked, gesturing to the drums. "Shouldn't we wait until we've won to celebrate? We should be getting weapons."

"It's not for revelry," a man snapped as he hurried past the two and onto the deck.

Akio waited for someone to explain, but no one seemed interested in providing any additional information. He stood awkwardly rooted to the spot, rubbing his fingers for comfort as he tried to figure out what to do. Mizuki started barking out orders as she positioned herself in front of the ōdaiko. Turning to ask Saori where he should go, Akio saw she vanished.

"Guess I'll just wait here," Akio said to no one in particular.

He scanned the deck, his attention being pulled in all directions by the well-organized chaos unfurling in front of him. Saori appeared next to Mizuki, her face set as she regripped her bachi. Mizuki's hair, no longer hung down her back. Instead, the short hair was tied in two tails, emphasizing her sharp cheek bones. Akio noted how she stared intently at the fast-approaching enemy ship. Continuing his search, Akio spied Taka and a handful of others behind the chū. The remaining crew stood at the ready, their weapons drawn.

The wind died down to barely a whisper, the waters stilling as if in anticipation for battle. Still, the Kingr with their raven flag drew closer. Time moved at a snail's pace. A bead of sweat ran down the side of Akio's face, not from the heat, but from the uneasy trepidation that left him full of energy that waited to be released.

Finally, the ship got close enough that Akio could properly see it and those onboard. The flag indeed bore the image of a raven, the thick dark outline of the bird rested inside what he imagined was the sun in the top left corner of the flag. The remainder was a crisp white. The flag flapped in the tiniest breath of wind, the massive longship's sail hanging limp in contrast. Akio's breath caught in his throat; the ship was massive. Long and thin, the longship was crafted from a dark wood. The prow had been carved into the head of a mighty lizard, possibly the Kingr's idea of what a dragon might look like. Akio might have found it all beautiful if it weren't for the situation.

A low rumbling note blasted from the longship. Standing tall and proud, a man with long golden hair blew a horn. Mixed with the ominous feelings that already swirled within him, the sound of the horn was one of war to Akio. War and death. The deep thrumming of song emanated from the enemy ship. Wordless but powerful. A beseechment to the gods for victory. Akio felt his legs buckle, but he managed to remain standing as his breathing quickened to match his racing heart.

"Hold steady," Toshio called out.

The words had a calming effect that surprised Akio. Though he still stood frozen in place, petrified by the approaching foe, a small wave of courage trickled down his back like warm water. The closer they came, the easier it was for Akio to observe the Kingr. The man who blew the warhorn stood much taller than Akio. He hoped it wouldn't come to hand-to-hand combat. The rest wore helms of crafted steel, the sun catching off them and limiting Akio's vision. They either wore a sort of armor or thick leather hides to protect their bodies. A few had painted their faces with black or blue paint, their eyes exposed to create the illusion of a demon.

Akio found his hands trembling, perspiration making his palms clammy.

The Kingr's song boomed louder the closer they came. Soon, Akio could make out some of their faces, specifically the whites of their eyes against the black paint. Many raised their axes over their heads, roaring out a war cry that muffled the song. The *Taihō* waited. Her crew stood positioned behind their drums, every soul standing tense with bated breath.

"Why don't they attack?" Akio cried in a strangled whisper. He danced in place, shaking his hands as they opened and closed as though he prepared to grip something. "Shit! Shit!"

Akio noticed that his panic distracted no one. Not a single head turned to observe his outburst. Still they waited.

IV

T HE SNAP OF THE KINGR'S FLAG cracked like a whip over the thunderous singing that emanated from their longship. The sails puffed out in a weak attempt to fill them as small gusts of wind failed to provide any sort of forward momentum for the ships. The longship pulled alongside the *Taihō*, the Kingr rushing up from below deck, their battleaxes waving in the air. Akio looked around, trying to locate anything that could be used as a weapon. A panicked curse escaped him, his voice squeaking out as all he could find was a length of rope. Akio spun to run to the heart of the *Taihō* hoping to grab one of the cooks' knives to arm himself with.

A solitary boom stopped him.

Turning slowly, Akio watched as Mizuki's arm moved gracefully, the bachi creating a line from tip to her torso. The dramatic angle caught Akio's attention, rooting him to the spot.

Don!

A second thunderous boom ran out as Mizuki struck the face of the drum. Akio thought he felt the ship dip in the water, his body listing sideways. Shouts from the Kingr filled the air, their chanting song stopping abruptly.

"Attack!" Toshio's shout cut through the cry of the Kingr. He dropped his arm in a sharp slicing motion as though he carried a sword.

Don! Don! Don!

Mizuki and Saori began beating the ōdaiko in perfect unison. Their strikes went through the drum, producing a deep, rich tone. Cries from the Kingr rang out once more, but the two did not stop. Then came the shime. The higher pitched rope drums played out a quick rhythm with a galloping beat before the chū finally joined in. Kingr rushed to the edge of the longship brandishing their weapons. Akio wondered why those aboard the *Taihō* didn't do the same. His body swayed side to side from the waves created by the two ships. However, no one else seemed to notice on the *Taihō*. The music rang in the air, powerful yet beautiful. Akio heard a loud crack, then more cries from the Kingr. They were different. They were pure terror.

Staggering as he fought to remain upright, Akio made his way to the edge of the ship. No one on the ship batted an eye as Akio wobbled between the drums and those standing at the ready with their weapons drawn. Akio noticed that as Taka and the others played, their energy and expression couldn't be more different from the days before. Their bodies moved with determined strength, striking the drums with powerful hits. Fire shone in Taka's eyes as he focused on the enemy longship. It was as though a phoenix were about to break free from his soul, answering his call.

The drummers hit another strike in unison with the ōdaiko. An ear-splitting crack rang in the air followed by more shouts. Akio's attention was ripped from the drummers and returned to the longship. Gasping in shock, Akio couldn't believe his eyes. Large cracks in the once majestic longship splintered the wood, almost snapping the ship in two. Men ran to the edges, clinging to the siding as those below deck struggled to turn the ship in retreat. Another ōdaiko note boomed in the air. Akio watched in horror as an unseen force raced towards the longship. The only sign of the attack was the trail it cut through the ocean. The energy slammed into the Kingr vessel causing the break to spider along the hull. A plume of ocean spray shot up from where the attack struck.

One of the Kingr toppled over the side into the roiling sea with a terrified shriek. His head broke through the spray for a moment, bobbing between the ships on the waves. Akio's stomach flipped and he quickly shied away as the waters brought the two ships together, their wooden frames slamming together with a shuddering crunch and throwing people on both sides to their knees. As Akio got back on his feet, he frantically scanned the seas looking for the fallen Kingr, but there was no sign of the golden-haired warrior.

A pang of pity filled Akio. He didn't know what he expected, but to be crushed between two boats had to be a painful way to go. Pain from fear and the actual impact – the idea overwhelmed him.

Deep cracks through the middle of the longship threatened to snap it in two. Kingr scrambled to turn it around, the oars beating furiously in retreat as shouts filled the air. The carved dragon head on the prow crumbled, the beast lost to the sea like her kin. As the longship turned from the *Taihō*, a final act of defiance in the form of a hail of arrows rained onto the *Taihō*. Cries of pain rang out as men were struck by the bolts. Akio jumped back, his heart racing as one dug itself neatly into the wood where he had been standing just moments before.

He strained to hear for a yelp of pain from Saori or Taka, his eyes still fixed on the retreating longship in case a second volley flew towards them. The raven flag flapped weakly during their escape, the tattered fabric leaving only the bird intact. By the time Akio felt safe, the image of the raven could no longer be seen, with only the damaged frame of the longship visible on the horizon.

Letting out a sigh of relief, Akio finally turned his attention to the *Taihō*. His gaze traveled the length of the ship to see who was injured. The drummers stopped playing, all but the ōdaiko as they beat out the last notes of battle. A wave of relief washed over Akio as he saw both Mizuki and Saori standing strong and untouched amidst the chaos. The feeling was short-lived as he knew others were not so lucky.

Those who stood by with their weapons drawn during the skirmish tended to the wounded. Buckets of water and clean clothes wiped and bandaged puncture wounds before they were wrapped. Small puddles of red stained the deck. It was a miracle there weren't more injured. Finding his feet, Akio walked the deck offering help where he thought he could, but being turned away each time. Men wheeled the drums down to the sleeping quarters in silence. Faces were set in grimaces as they worked to clean the deck. Akio managed to locate Taka as the man returned from below deck.

"Yamamoto!" Akio called out. In the deafening silence, Akio felt awkward breaking it, as though he were disrespecting the efforts of those who fought that day.

Taka made his way to Akio, the younger man standing frozen after his outburst. Seeing Taka approach comforted Akio a little. His friend also appeared to be unharmed as well.

"Come with me," Taka said quietly.

This solemn Taka unnerved Akio, but he didn't protest. The two made their way to the other side of the *Taihō*, away from the bustle of the cleanup. Even here, there were still people milling about, looking as uneasy as Akio no doubt did.

"What's going on?" Akio asked, keeping his voice down.

"Senchou was hit," Taka replied. "We don't have proper materials, but they're stitching him up as best they can."

Akio's jaw dropped.

"Those bastards got a good number of us," Taka continued. "Got Shigeru and Watanabe too." Taka gnashed his teeth and balled his fists.

"I saw Satō was hit too," Akio said softly. "And more. Why did they attack us?"

Taka slammed his fist against the side of the ship, causing Akio to jump. The man began pacing in a small circle, gaze cast down as he walked. This angry Taka unnerved Akio. A rage simmered deep within. Akio wondered how much was truly a part of Taka as he remembered the intensity of his glare during the battle. Was the jovial Taka a mask? Akio pushed the thoughts away for now. Clearly, Taka took his friends' injuries hard and was beating himself up. Then there was Toshio. Failing to protect the captain was the utmost disgrace. Akio hadn't even been fighting, yet he felt the weight of his inaction. Would Toshio's death be on his head?

"Did you see Senchou?" Akio asked, trying to refocus.

Taka shook his head. The question got him to stop pacing as he struggled with his thoughts. Akio watched the internal turmoil, wondering if he should say anything or if he should leave Taka's battle undisturbed.

"When I went to clean up," Taka said breaking the silence, "I saw the backs of our those working on the injured. We don't have healers or anything. Just those who know how to sew. We've learned skin can be covered with stitches too.

"Anyway, there were hurried whispers and lots of bloody rags. And smoke." The last part came as almost an afterthought as Taka's voice took on a soft, pensive quality. His gaze turned inward as he recalled something. "Not tobacco, but something lightly scented."

Akio's face fell. He knew that scent well. It filled his home after his grandfather died.

Akio's voice trembled as he asked, "Do you think he will make it?" The thought of the old man succumbing to his wounds brought tears to his eyes. Akio gulped, fighting the lump forming in his throat. "It can't be that bad, can it?"

He hoped not.

"I don't know," Taka replied. "They'll do their best."

The two stood apart, lost in their thoughts. Tears rolled down Akio's cheeks and blurred his vision. He couldn't bear the notion that Toshio could die. Memories of his grandfather filled his mind. The tears, everyone dressed in black after changing from the white of the funeral, and the empty house. The silence had been the worst. His grandfather's house had always been filled with noise, whether it was from one of Grandma's dramas blaring on the television or one of Grandpa's records playing old jazz, the needle skipping over the ridges and creating a staticky scratch. Even the chaotic chirping from their songbirds out back disappeared when he died. There had been so much life. After he died, Grandma got rid of the birds, got rid of the records, and stopped watching her shows. She would only sit in her chair in silence, a framed picture of her and Grandpa on the little table next to her.

Akio couldn't bear to lose another grandfather. His own grandfather left too soon, before Akio could learn everything he needed to know. He couldn't lose someone else before they told him they were proud of him. Mumbled words caused Akio's grandfather's home to disappear. Blinking through the tears, Akio attempted to focus on what was being said.

"What?" he asked through the lump in his throat.

"I'm going back to see if there's any news on Senchou or the others," Taka repeated. "Are you coming?"

Akio turned to face the sea. A warm breeze played across his face, drying his tears. There hadn't been a breeze in a few days. If he wasn't so distraught, it would be pleasant.

"I think I'll stay here for a bit. Thank you."

Taka didn't reply, but his vanishing footsteps let Akio know that he was alone. Placing both hands on the side of the *Taihō*, Akio took a deep breath, savoring the tangy salt. It was a beautiful day despite the heat, and yet he struggled to find the beauty.

V

WHITE SEA SPRAY SHOT into the air as water hit the hull. The white caps of waves rolled into the pristine blue waters. The sea was the absolute perfect shade of blue, azure like the cloudless sky. The combination of gentle rocking, tangy sea air, and crystalline beauty produced a soothing, hypnotic effect on Akio. Painful memories and uncertainty were washed away and replaced with serenity. Closing his eyes, Akio allowed himself to be lost in the moment.

On the deck of the *Taihō*, Akio no longer stood, bound to his physical body. Instead, he felt himself traveling through time, just floating through the void. A sense of lightness filled him and he could almost feel his toes leave the ship. Brilliant colors flashed in his mind's eye as though he looked through a prism. Then the world went dark. Tiny pinpricks broke through the blackness – stars shining in the heavens. A light aroma tingled his nostrils, but Akio couldn't quite identify it.

Focusing on the scent, Akio found it getting stronger. Excitement filled him as he came closer to recognizing the mystery smell.

A moment later it was as though a bubble popped. The familiar aroma disappeared and the salty tang returned. The colors, stars, and blackness were gone, replaced by the red orange that comes when the sun hits closed eyelids. A feeling of profound loss washed over Akio and he couldn't figure out why. He had been so close to identifying the smell. Could it actually be disappointment at the loss? Opening his eyes, Akio stared out into the vast expanse. His mind wandered aimlessly, trying to make sense of the strange experience he just had. Why did it matter? Why did he need the answer? What was he even trying to figure out?

A fish breached the water, its wriggling body shining over the azure waves as the sun flashed off its scales. It proved to be a welcome distraction. Allowing his attention to wander, Akio scanned the horizon. Waves lazily pushed forward in the sea, their white caps providing the only change to the still blue. As he was about to lose himself to his thoughts once more, something caught his eye. In the distance, a pod of dolphins played. The majestic creatures jumped out of the waters. Akio's spirits began to soar, just like the dolphins. He'd never seen any before. He felt giddy like a child.

Resting his arms on the ship's side, Akio let himself relax as he observed the dolphins frolicking. They must have noticed the *Taihō* because they gradually made their way towards the ship in a zigzagging pattern. When they cut through the water, Akio saw how powerful they were. The waves helped propel them forward, their streamlined bodies cutting a swath through the sea and leaving a trail of bubbles in their wake. Akio sighed, envious of their freedom.

"You're jealous, aren't you?"

Saori rested her elbows on the ship's gunwale beside him and stared into the vast ocean. Assuming she spoke about the dolphins, he nodded. The two watched the dolphins play next to the *Taihō* in silence. A few members of the pod jumped and spun, breaking through the waves in graceful displays of acrobatics.

"I wonder what it's like to be free," Saori sighed, a sigh on her lips as she watched the dolphins. "To just go wherever your heart wants to."

The sunlight made her eyes sparkle despite the longing on her face. Her furrowed brows hinted at some hidden sorrow within. A gust of wind hit the two of them, a sheet of her hair flying in her face and obscuring her vision momentarily. She reminded Akio so much of someone, but he could quite place it. How long until he could finally remember?

"It seems pretty relaxed on here," Akio said, motioning to the *Taihō*.

"It is," she agreed. "But we're not truly free."

Her cryptic words hit Akio hard. There was something odd to them, but he could sense the truth in them as well. Saori met his gaze momentarily before turning back to the sea. He remembered his conversation with Taka earlier.

"What's going on?"

Akio didn't expect the question to be so blunt now that the emotions from the battle had died down. Saori faced him, her eyes studying his – reading something that lay hidden. He felt the blood rush to his cheeks as he uncomfortably shifted his gaze, looking down at his feet.

"I wish they told you when you first arrived," Saori murmured. She lifted her hand and moved a bit of hair from his eyes. "Most don't know. They're not ready to remember." Her voice soothed his nerves. The change from her usual timbre brought butterflies to his stomach.

"Know what?" he gulped, his voice almost a whisper.

Saori's mood shifted, her body shrinking as she held herself. Akio's butterflies went crazy as he saw someone whom he believed to be powerful close in on herself so quickly until she reminded him of a child. On instinct, he moved forward to comfort her, but Saori shook her head so minutely that Akio wondered if she even noticed she did it. Her attention darted from one side of the ship to the other, taking in everyone nearby. Akio followed suit, noting that they were alone. He wondered when the others left.

"Please don't talk about this," Saori begged, releasing her self-hug and rubbing her hands together. "I don't want to ruin it for the others."

"Ruin what?"

"Have you ever wondered why everyone is so carefree on here?"

The question resonated in Akio's mind. He replayed his time on the ship, his interactions with the others. Taka especially came to the forefront. The dichotomy between his earlier demeanor and the usual easygoing attitude stood out to Akio. Their previous conversation and his actions were deeply troubling. He allowed his mind to move out, evaluating the other members of the *Taihō*'s crew. He remembered how they would walk away, perplexed, whenever he asked about their past, and how they seemed to not recollect the conversation just hours later. Everything flowed with a happy-go-lucky attitude, as freely as the alcohol had during their previous celebrations. Of the group, Satō stood out. He was known to party with Taka and the others, but Akio also recalled the man spending time by himself. Appearing to be in his early forties, Satō was among the older members of the crew.

Saori must have seen the realization dawn on his face because hers switched from nervous to pity. Her hand reached out and gently grabbed his. A thrill went through Akio's body at her light touch. Despite constantly using her hands for taiko and chores, her fingers were soft and delicate.

"Satō-san," Akio said. "And Senchou. He seemed to want to tell me something."

"And a few others," Saori added. "Yamada-sama for sure. Definitely Senchou. I feel sorry for the both of them."

"How long have Senchou and Satō-san been here?"

Saori thought for a moment, her nose crinkling. "I want to say that Senchou has been here for at least eighty years. Satō-san's been here the longest. I don't think even he remembers when he first joined anymore."

Akio's jaw dropped. The man looked no older than his mid-forties. He spoke and acted like those Akio knew back home. But from what Saori said, he should be dead. The same for Toshio. Their captain was already elderly. How could he have an additional eighty years on him?

"That doesn't make sense." His tone held both conviction and confusion, reflecting his inner turmoil. "How can someone live that long?"

Akio's mind raced. A thousand questions vied for his attention. How could they be so old, but look and act so young? How come no one else noticed? Saori said earlier that he reminded her of herself. Why?

"What happened with the Kingr?"

His mind made a decision.

Saori's mouth opened and closed a few times before she managed to compose an answer. "The Kingr and the Zhōnghuá have been our enemies for ages," she explained. "Both seek Ryū-ō. Our guess is that the Kingr enjoy the hunt and are hoping to best the god. I don't think they actually understand that he is a god though. They want the glory of slaying a mighty beast. The Zhōnghuá, I believe, seek the mighty dragon for religious and medicinal purposes. From what I understand, their lore has a similar dragon. So, they may believe he follows their stories. Ryū-ō must be protected from both. He is our god."

"And the battle?" Akio pressed. "Their ship was destroyed while we just played a menacing song. What the hell?"

"Ah," Saori replied with a smile. "Our taiko are more than they seem. Blessed by the gods long ago, our music helps protect us as we continue our sacred journey. The beats give us power."

"To destroy ships?" Incredulity dripped from his voice.

He was greeted with a nod of agreement which only confused him more.

"Okay, so I'm on a magical boat where people don't age, with laser cannon drums, all while we hunt a literal dragon god. Got it."

A solitary tear rolled down Saori's cheek. The unusual display of emotion by her dampened his indignation, turning to concern.

"I'm sorry," he stuttered, feeling awkward. "It just sounds so farfetched, you know? But please, what's going on?"

The loud *don* of the ōdaiko startled them. Akio could see Mizuki striking the drum. The crew gathered around her, emerging from below deck.

"We should go," Saori said with a sniffle. She moved past him to join the throng.

"Wait!" Akio grabbed her wrist. "Tell me. Please. I need to know what's going on."

Saori's lip trembled as her breath came out in a shudder. Wiping her eyes, Saori set her face into her usual nonchalant expression. The booming beats continued in the background, and Saori turned to join the others. With a sigh, Akio followed. As they neared the group, Akio's mind raced once more. His conversation with Saori only brought more questions. A light touch on his hand halted the chaos in his mind. Saori stopped short of the cluster. Her face went pale, but her expression was set. Akio opened his mouth, but she silenced him with a shake of her head.

"We're dead."

VI

AKIO'S HEAD SPUN as he and Saori joined the group. She continued to hold his hand up until they reached the edge of the crowd. How could she drop a bomb on him like that and not say anything else? Mizuki continued to strike the drum, calling for the crew together for a meeting. The remaining members made their way over, emerging from all corners of the ship.

Dead. How could they all be dead? His lungs filled with air. He ate and slept. He could touch everything, his hands not slipping through as though he held no corporeal form. He even felt pain when he kicked his toe against a door frame the other day. How? There was even blood when they'd been shot. How? His stomach knotted in confusion. Images of Satō lying on the deck, an arrow embedded in his thigh and blood pooling around him flit through Akio's mind. He recalled the grimace of agony on Satō's face. The dead don't feel pain.

"Fuck," Akio murmured.

Next to him Watanabe elbowed him gently, a bandage wrapped around his arm from where the arrow struck him earlier. All things considered, he seemed to be in good shape. Watanabe must have heard Akio just then.

"Don't worry, Katō," Watanabe whispered. "I'm sure we'll get good news. Good thoughts."

Unsure what to say, Akio nodded with a feeble smile. The pair turned their attention back to Mizuki who positioned herself for one last strike. As the final note reverberated in the air, a hush fell over the ship. Akio found himself holding his breath, waiting for Mizuki to speak.

Mizuki faced the crowd, her hands now behind her back. Akio watched her scan the group. Her brows knit together as she brought her hands from behind her back, clapping them together once as she spoke.

"My friends," Mizuki's mousy voice cut clear in the silence. "I have good news. Our dear captain is now resting. Those who tended to him and the other injured have told me that their wounds have been cleaned and stitched up. Our family will be whole once more."

A cheer broke out from the crowd. Akio felt a wave of relief wash over him at the thought of Toshio recovering, pushing his confusion from Saori's revelation out of his mind for now. Mizuki raised her hands and a hush fell over the crowd once more.

"I want to thank you all for your efforts. Without all of our combined efforts, we would not have been able to rebuff the Kingr. Thank you."

Mizuki dipped into a deep bow. She held the pose for several long seconds before straightening up. Akio felt a bit of pride swell within. Despite not having taken part in the skirmish, no one had treated him so kindly before. He almost felt shame at being unable to be helpful. He didn't deserve such respect. It felt nice to be appreciated.

"We will take the next few weeks to rest," Mizuki continued. "But we must still be on guard. The Kingr may have retreated, but the Zhōnghuá sail these waters as well. We mustn't become complacent."

"Will we still seek out Ryū-ō?" a voice called out from the crowd.

"Not at this time," Mizuki replied. "It is Senchou's desire that we do not harass the mighty dragon. The god has given us two gifts this day: victory and his protection by safeguarding our crew. We will honor the god and leave him in peace for now. Never fear," Mizuki added after a pause after seeing several people in front of Akio begin to express their displeasure. "We will still pursue Ryū-ō. Senchou just wants to pay proper respect to the god."

Bowing once more in thanks to the crew, Mizuki turned and disappeared back into the heart of the ship. Once she was gone, the crowd gradually dispersed. Akio turned to Saori, wanting to continue their discussion, but she'd vanished. Spinning around in confusion, he tried to find her but she was nowhere to be found. Not wanting to speak with Taka or the others, Akio wandered off in hopes of finding a quiet spot on the ship to collect his thoughts.

His feet carried him around the deck multiple times until he found a nice little corner. Gazing into the sea, Akio hoped to spot the dolphins once more even though he knew they were long gone. The ocean lost its magic, the sparkling sun on its crystalline surface no longer holding his attention. The salty sea air was no longer refreshing as it once had been. With a sigh, Akio slumped to the deck, pulling his knees to his chest and resting his forehead on top.

"It doesn't make sense," he said to his knees. "How can I be dead?"

Akio tried to remember his life prior to his time on the *Taihō*. Flashes of his childhood, a flood of emotions following close after, filled his mind. He remembered his grandfather, his sister, Miyako, and his girlfriend, Yumi. Miyako always tried to spend time with him when they were younger. After a long day at school and after school classes, all Akio wanted was to slough off his clothes and melt into bed. When he came home, however, Miyako waited for him, an ice cream cone in each hand. As he neared the front door, she jumped up and ran to him, pressing the treat into his hand. It tasted wonderful and the two ate their snack before heading in. Stars were shining. His little sister was resting her head on his shoulder. But he couldn't see her face. Why? Akio could taste the ice cream, but he couldn't see her.

Just like he hadn't been able to conjure up Yumi's face.

"What the fuck?" he gasped. In frustration, Akio began hitting his head with the palm of his hand. "Why?"

A strangled sob of anger caught in his throat. All he wanted was to scream, but Akio didn't want to draw attention to himself. Instead, he bit his knuckles. Hot tears rolled down his cheeks, ignored. Akio sat for a long time like this, his tears dampening his pants to the point that he had little moist splotches on his knees. He didn't know if anyone saw him. If they did, they left him alone. When Akio's emotions finally settled down, he lifted his tear-stained face. He sat completely exhausted, his body empty of emotion after all he'd just experienced.

"Damn," he whispered, rubbing his face with the back of his arm. "I'm fucking dead."

He didn't want to believe it, but realization started sinking in. He couldn't remember his life right before boarding the *Taihō*. He had to be ready for the possibility that he truly was dead.

"Do you know?"

The sudden question startled Akio. Next to him, like a master of stealth, Satō managed to make his way to the side of the ship without Akio hearing him.

"Do you know?" Satō repeated.

With a nod, Akio moved to stand up, but Satō motioned for him to remain seated. Maneuvering his bandaged leg, Satō groaned as he took a seat next to Akio. Dull red bled through the white sheets that bandaged Satō's leg. Akio tried not to stare, but found the wound too hard to pull his gaze from.

"I'm sorry," Satō said, his apology surprising Akio. "You don't deserve this."

"What happened?" Akio asked for the third time that day. "Why does no one else know?"

"Some do. Most haven't woken up yet. You're right though – well, Inoue-chan, right? You two talk?"

Akio nodded.

"Poor girl," Satō sighed. "She's had it rough too. They all do, those who find out early."

"How can we be dead?" Akio asked.

"The *Taihō* is a home to lost souls," Satō began. "A place for those who died before their time."

"Was I hit by a car?" Akio blurted out in a panic. His hands went to his body, feeling for broken bones that would not be there.

"No, no, son," Satō said, patting Akio's knee. "It's not that simple. We all ended our own lives."

Akio was about to protest, but a wave of horror and understanding washed over him. The overwhelming emotions strangled his already exhausted body, making it difficult to breathe. At the same time, he saw himself sitting at his kitchen table, his work clothes hanging disheveled on his frame, and a bottle of umeshu in his hand. On the counter, several bottles stood empty, one resting on its side, the neck hanging over the edge. Like Akio.

At twenty-three, life as an office worker left him feeling unsatisfied. Every day it was the same thing – wake up, go to work, come home. He worked hard to help Yumi pay for university so she could realize her dream of becoming a pediatrician, but that meant long hours and very little time to see each other. As the days blurred together into one of endless loneliness, Akio began drinking. On more than one occasion, he woke up slumped over his kitchen table, a blanket draped over him and the bottles cleaned up.

Each day got harder than the last. The bills piled up, bills he'd hid from Yumi so she wouldn't see. It wouldn't be fair to stress her out when she only had a year left before medical school. So he kept working. And kept drinking.

Akio's eyes burned as tears spilled out. He suddenly remembered it all so clearly. When the umeshu bottle was empty he made his way to his room to grab a warm jacket. It was a good night for a walk. He found himself at his old high school. Somehow, he found himself on the roof, staring out at the yard below. The air was crisp and he was glad he brought the jacket. He thought about his parents and friends. He remembered Miyako and her sweet smile.

Akio gasped as he could finally see all their faces. A sob escaped him as he saw his mother and sister. Soon, he would see Yumi.

As the memory continued, he saw her. Long lashes framed her mesmerizing brown eyes. Her smile was so warm and dazzling, it could melt snow. He remembered her touch and how his body tingled each time their flesh met. Her bell-like laugh elicited a shuddering sob, the specific memory of Yumi causing her to clutch his arm in her mirth. He couldn't do it. Akio slipped off the ledge. There was no relief as his feet touched the roof. His stomach still clenched as their overwhelming debt pushed away all traces of Yumi. Soon, the collectors would come. He failed her and there was only one way to fix it. The letter would explain it all, and inform her of the life insurance policy.

Before he could change his mind, Akio spun around felt the ground disappear beneath him. The wind whipped through his hair as tears ran down his cheeks. He hoped Yumi would forgive him. Miyako too. Regret overwhelmed him, but it was too late.

"Oh god," Akio whispered as his memories faded to black. "I remember."

Panic gripped Akio and his chest tightened. Satō placed his hand on Akio's back, comforting the distressed young man.

"I'm sorry," Satō soothed. "The first time is the hardest, but it doesn't get easier either."

"I jumped off my high school's roof so my girlfriend could have my life insurance money." Akio didn't know why he felt the need to explain, but the words forced their way past his lips. "She must be so hurt. And my sister. I probably broke my sister's heart."

"They most likely were hurt, but they loved you. One thing you learn is that it's never as bad as we think it is – until it's too late. It's a hard lesson to accept."

"How did you -?" Akio blurted out. Instantly, he was hit with regret. "I'm so sorry."

"No, it's fine. I hanged myself. My wife left me and took my kids back to her parents. I was alone, and it seemed easier to end my grief than live alone." Satō sighed, pinching the bridge of his nose. "I wish I thought of the impact it would have on my children."

The two sat in silence, Akio collecting his thoughts. He assumed Satō was doing the same. Satō rubbed his hands, his attention focused elsewhere. Akio felt a twang a pity for the man. He'd clearly been through a lot.

"How long have you been on the *Taihō*?" Akio asked.

Satō didn't face Akio as he began speaking. "It's been ninety-six years." His voice came out slow and deliberate. "I've seen Ryū-ō four times. Four people were blessed. Never me. I'm tired." Satō's sudden change in affect caught Akio off-guard. He stood up and faced the now setting sun. "I don't think I can keep waiting. I've made it further than most. That counts for something, right?"

The two locked gazes, Akio slowly standing. Something about Satō's tone made him uneasy.

"Take care of yourself, Akio." The use of his name in such a personal manner didn't help Akio's apprehension. "Don't beat yourself up for past mistakes. I know you're a good kid. Ryū-ō's blessing is real. You have a good chance."

"Please, don't." Akio wasn't sure what Satō could do, but his dread kept rising. "Whatever it is, we can fix it together."

Climbing onto the ledge, Satō shook his head with a wan smile. "It was nice meeting you, Akio."

"Satō-san," Akio muttered, his voice cracking as he reached out to the man.

"Yūto. Call me Yūto. Take care of yourself. Good-bye."

Before Akio could react, Satō leaned back and fell into the sea. The waves lapped around him, their waters appearing red in the light of the setting sun. Resting on his back, Akio could make out a smile of relief on Satō's face. White foam framed his head like a pillow, and he folded his hands across his chest. The waters splashed over him, carrying him from the *Taihō* until he drifted out of sight.

A lump welled in Akio's throat as tears rolled down his cheeks once more. He stood rooted to the spot until the sun completely set and darkness blanketed him. Until it hid Satō from the world. The night comforted him, letting Akio hide his pain. How many like Satō gave up on this second chance to live aboard the *Taihō* until blessed by the sea dragon god?

"I wonder if he'll see his children again?" Akio murmured. "I wonder if I'll ever see Yumi or Miyako."

Sounds of merriment emanated from the helm. Akio spun and saw people dancing around a fire. They were probably celebrating the captain's recovery and their victory from earlier that day. Though he didn't feel like partaking in the festivities, Akio found himself walking towards the revelry.

VII

Despite it having been a hot day, the temperature had already dropped considerably and the wind picked up, prickling Akio's skin. The fire proved to be most welcome as heat from the flames warmed him nicely. A few men played the chappa and uchiwa daiko, the brassy clang of the hand cymbals accenting the fan-like hand drum. Sake flowed, cups being thrust into empty hands. Yet there was a somber tone that lay in the background behind the merriment.

Throwing his head back, Akio downed his drink, shoving the empty cup in someone's hand as he walked by. Dancers wove their way through the many bodies on deck, their movements not as exuberant as the last time. Akio scanned the crowd in search of Saori. To his surprise, he saw Taka standing off to the side nursing his drink. Seeing his friend abstaining from the festivities and alone concerned him.

Making his way to his friend, Akio called out to Taka. The man lifted his head, recognition dawning on his face a moment later. Giving Akio a weak smile, Taka took a sip and returned to staring at his cup.

"Everything okay?" Akio asked gently pushing Taka's cup hand down.

"Yeah," Taka mumbled not looking up.

Confusion crossed Taka's face, followed by sadness as though he were trying to reconcile his feelings. Akio saw a lot of himself in Taka at that moment.

"Want to talk?"

There was a moment of silence. Taka opened his mouth as though he wanted to say something but didn't know where to start.

"I – uh – I think I just had a bad dream," Taka mumbled. "I was having a hard time with everything. Senchou is like a father to me. Seeing him hurt like that just scared me, so I took a nap. I dreamt that I was walking down a dark road. I must've been celebrating something because I felt a little drunk. Then these two lights were barreling towards me. I woke up with my heart racing. I know it's just a dream, but it felt so real. God, it felt so real."

Taka pressed his palm into his face. Akio braced himself in case his friend tried to do anything else, like Satō. He wondered if he should tell Taka the truth.

"Have you had dreams like that before?"

Taka shook his head. Akio didn't have it in his heart to say anything at that moment. Maybe it was a one-time incident. If he had another Akio would tell him.

"Don't let it bother you," Akio said, rubbing his friend's shoulder. "It's been a crazy day. It's probably just stress." Putting on a smile, Akio gave Taka a little push. "Come on. Let's relax a little. We deserve it."

Taka hesitated, glancing down at his empty cup and back to the festivities. Longing filled his eyes, and Akio could almost feel the internal struggle within his friend. He tried so hard to keep the pity off his face. It wouldn't help Taka and probably make things worse. Confirming Taka's thoughts would break the normally easygoing man. No, it was better for Akio to lie and keep his discovery to himself. Until he found Saori anyways. Handing his cup to Akio, Taka attempted to put on a smile as he moved to join the others. The action brought peace to Akio, but he could see how Taka still struggled.

The pair blended in with the others. Akio made sure not to consume anymore alcohol, but he didn't stop Taka from drowning his sorrows until his happy-go-lucky spirit returned. It took a while, but eventually Taka found himself an uchiwa and began beating a peppy rhythm with the others. On more than one occasion, Taka and the others inquired about Satō. Akio's stomach clenched, but he held his tongue. He didn't want to say anything until after he spoke to Saori.

Their celebrations lasted long into the night. They feasted on the squid they'd seen earlier, having caught it right before the Kingr were spotted. Akio tried to find out who captured it, but no one seemed to know. He savored every morsel of the squid. It reminded him of his mother's cooking, something he'd never managed to replicate. As he snacked, Akio caught glimpses of his childhood – as though he was being transported back in time. He wandered through the kitchen, savoring the aroma of his mother's cooking. Her favorite fragrance wafted in the air as though she just passed by. In the distance, Akio swore he could hear her call out to him. She was so close, just in the other room. Akio's heart ached. He wanted to see her – to apologize for what he did and hug her.

"I'm here!" Akio called out.

"Katō!" Watanabe's voice replied.

The kitchen vanished and Akio's heart sank. He could still smell her perfume. Attempting to mask his disappointment, Akio turned to Watanabe.

"Put down your drink," Watanabe said with a jovial slap to the back. "You're totally out of it. Come, we're going to write a new song to celebrate our victory over the Kingr."

Still mourning his lost chance to finally see his mother one more time, Akio followed his friend, intrigued nonetheless. As they made their way towards the fire, Akio caught a glimpse of Saori. She stood off to the side, drink in hand and bouncing to the beat of the chappa and uchiwa. She looked so happy, her hair fanning out as she spun around. Akio tried to catch her eye, but he didn't know if she saw him. He made a note to find her once he'd gotten some rest.

Watanabe led Akio over to Taka and a few others. They each had an uchiwa in hand. Akio observed the group, noticing that they were the main members of the crew who played the chū during the battle with the Kingr. Satō's absence left a pit in Akio's stomach. To his dismay, Satō's name was never brought up again, almost as though he never existed.

It took a while, but the group came up with an upbeat song with a swing beat. Akio couldn't help but get caught up in the song. Eventually, they handed him an uchiwa. Akio felt honored they trusted him so much and vowed to do his best to not disappoint them once the song was translated to the chū. Despite everything, he had a nagging feeling in the back of his mind that he was replacing Satō.

VIII

RUBBING THE SLEEP OUT of his eyes, Akio got up. Though he barely drank, he was the last one up again. The sleeping quarters were empty, their blankets and pillows all put neatly away. With a yawn, Akio stretched before getting up. They'd stayed up into the early hours of the morning practicing the new song and Akio felt exhausted. The emotional extremes he'd experienced didn't help.

Blinding sunlight caused his eyes to throb as he threw up his arm with a groan. Even without a hangover, he felt miserable. Dreams of Satō's final moments plagued Akio, making sleep next to impossible. He wondered if Satō could even die again or if he was doomed to float for eternity upon the waves. Akio hadn't fully accepted that he was dead; any thoughts of his past were pushed away. He needed to sort things out before he could move forward.

Breakfast continued as usual. Men chatted as they ate, a few sporting strips of cloth wrapped around various body parts. Other than that, nothing seemed amiss. No alarm had been sounded for Satō. It was like they truly forgot he existed. Standing in line to pick up his food, Akio searched for signs of the captain. His injuries sounded the most severe. He'd also been replaying their conversation, and Akio was pretty sure Toshio knew the truth as well.

"Come with me," a voice said behind him.

Akio nearly yelped as he spun to face Saori. "What the hell?" he gasped, but she was already leading him by the hand to a quiet spot.

The pair settled down atop some sake barrels. Saori took a few bites giving Akio time to do the same. The food felt nice and hot in his empty stomach. However, he missed the squid from the night before. He missed his mother's cooking. He hadn't eaten at home in almost a year.

"What happened to Satō?"

"Why do you think we spoke?" Akio asked. Somehow, his conversation with their crewmate felt private, and shouldn't be shared, even though he trusted Saori.

"I see it in your eyes. You know what happened."

Her eyes bored into his, probing for the answer. Akio felt his palms become clammy as he debated telling her the truth. There was no reason not to say anything, as she had explained so much. But somehow, the two imparting the private details of their deaths to each other felt too intimate to disclose. He had to do it though. With Satō gone, there was one less person who could answer his questions on the ship.

Gulping back the lump in his throat, Akio explained his final moments with Satō. How Satō helped him recall his last memories and the man's kind words to him before jumping overboard. Akio did not include any information about either of their deaths. It just didn't feel right at that moment. Saori stared into her bowl of soup, a darkness crossing her visage.

"He finally did it," she muttered.

The news struck Akio. "He'd talked about it before?"

Saori nodded. "I overheard him talking to Mizuki and Senchou years ago. They talked him out of it at the time, but I guess he never truly got over the idea. Damn."

"How? How can we die if we're already dead?"

"No one knows," she replied with a sigh. "I assume you're rejecting this second chance and allowing your spirit to disappear, but there's no one I can ask, right? Just like dying. No one knows."

Picking at her shirt, Saori dropped her gaze. Akio noticed that it was the same one Satō had when they last spoke. His heart dropped. How common was it to give up on eternal life?

"He wasn't the first, was he?" Akio asked. His words came out slowly, unsure if he should ask the question. It felt so distasteful and left a bitter taste in his mouth.

He was met with a nod. Saori's gaze never left the spot on her shirt as she continued to pick at it. Akio waited, staring at her intently. Something about her led him to believe she wanted to say something. The silence stretched on, and Akio gave her time to collect her thoughts. Finally, he was rewarded when she gave a mighty sigh, her fingers still pulling on the clothes.

"I remember one more person, but I'm sure there's many more. I have an idea how old the *Taihō* is. Well, two if you count Emi. Emi was on the *Taihō* right before you arrived. She hadn't even been here long. Maybe five years or so. She spent her first four years happy like everyone else. That last year though, I don't know what triggered it, but something in her snapped and she spent a year tormented by her final memories. You could see the change. Well, if you wanted to. You know how oblivious they all are. It's all just music and drinking with them until they remember. Watching her deterioration was heartbreaking.

"When I first came on, there was an old woman we just called Baa-chan. She was really sweet, especially to me. She would hold me at night when I couldn't sleep and sing softly to me. She was so special and I never got her name." Saori's voice dropped to almost a whisper. Her gaze stayed down, but Akio could see the tears dripping off her nose. "Baa-chan was everyone's grandma. I think she'd been here the longest, but Senchou and Satō-san had as well."

Her voice cracked and Akio just waited. He didn't try and stop her ramblings. It felt important that she got this off her chest. He didn't think she had anyone to talk to, not even Mizuki. Saori gave herself a couple minutes, sniffling a little before she continued.

"One day, Baa-chan pulled me aside. We walked around the deck of the *Taihō* for hours. Sometimes she would tell me about her past, but she mostly just listened to me. I remember we talked about how the flowers would bloom outside my parents' house every spring. The rain would wash away the snow and then the flowers would open up. Pinks, oranges, purples, and yellows. They were so beautiful. I miss them so much. Apparently, we lived in the same prefecture.

"The sun was setting by the time we finished. It was stunning. Like a picture. And Baa-chan said – she said..." Saori's voice trailed off as she was once again fighting back a sob. "She told me she loved me. How I made her time on the *Taihō* special." Tears now spilled down her cheeks. "She cupped my face," Saori's hands went to her cheeks, delicately touching the phantom hands she have felt. "'Be strong,' she said. 'Your day will come.' Then she hugged me tight. We went to bed like normal, Baa-chan stroking my hair to help me sleep. When I woke up, she was gone."

Their eyes met and Akio's heart broke at the agony he saw on her face. She looked like a little girl, lost and scared. Her lips trembled as she tried to blink away her tears. In a sudden unexpected motion, Akio pulled Saori into a hug. His hand rested gently on the back of her head as she cried on his shoulder. She felt so small.

"No one acknowledged she was gone," Saori sobbed. "Like she never existed. How?"

Unsure of what to say, Akio stroked her hair as he attempted to formulate an answer.

"You remember her." Akio stumbled through his words. "You made her last moments special. That's more than most can ask for on here, I think. Look at Satō-san. Those he was close with don't even remember. It's almost like we're cursed on this ship. Cursed to forget our lives. Our loved ones. Even our own."

Sniffling, Saori met his gaze. Understanding dawned on her face. Akio continued on, sorting out his own thoughts as he spoke.

"That's the trade-off. And when we manage to remember because we won't live in ignorance forever, it shatters whatever magic the *Taihō* has and breaks the illusion of happiness."

As he spoke, Akio felt like he was connecting the pieces of a puzzle. A sense of rightness tingled within him, as though the *Taihō* were telling him he was on the right track. Through his concentration, Akio noticed Saori watching him, intrigued. Akio briefly wondered if she went down the same path he did. Inside the back of his mind, Akio felt something tickling his brain, wanting to get discovered. Perhaps it wasn't a curse, but a punishment. Punishment for what though? Every soul on the *Taihō* was dead. At least three were by their own hand, though Taka's might have been an accident.

Did Toshio know? His speech right before their fight against the Kingr was almost exactly like the one he gave the day Akio first boarded the ship. Surely, the captain would know more about this magical ship?

"How did you die?" Akio asked on a hunch.

"I drowned myself in the stream by my grandparents' house." Saori's brow twitched up as she tried to figure out where he was going. "You?"

"I jumped off my high school roof so my girlfriend could get my life insurance money."

"Just for the money?" A faint accusatory tone tinged the question.

Shame flooded Akio as he remembered the scene of him sitting in his kitchen surrounded by alcohol. It was now his turn to drop his gaze.

"Not exactly," he mumbled. "I think I'd been thinking about it for a while. But I didn't want her to struggle while she was in school. I guess I didn't plan as well as I thought."

A hollow pit replaced the shame as Saori hugged him tight. Her tears dripping on to his neck only enhanced the emotion. The two held each other for a long while until Saori broke away with a sniffle, her eyes puffy and red.

"So, what does this all mean?" she finally asked.

"I think... I need to know how the others died," Akio said slowly.

"Why?"

"Because at least four of us killed ourselves. Maybe not Taka, but I can't shake off the feeling he was always a heavy drinker."

"Did he drink himself to death?" Saori asked, her usual snark tinging her words through her tears.

"No," Akio said with a heavy shake of his head. "I think he walked in front of a car while drunk."

"I can see that," Saori replied with a thoughtful expression. "I'm trying to think if Baa-chan ever said anything. I don't really remember."

"I'm wondering if that's part of the curse. We live for eternity as our punishment for killing ourselves? Doesn't seem like much of a damnation."

As Akio continued to process his thoughts, the tickling at the back of his mind cleared. It was as if he walked through a tunnel and was greeted by a blinding light.

"How often have you seen Ryū-ō?"

"Uh, I never have. I *think* Yamada-sama's seen him once or twice. Why?"

"What's his gift? What happens?" Excitement swirled inside him as he believed he was nearing the answer. It was as though something pulled him towards these questions, guiding his line of thought.

"I don't remember." The sudden realization that she had gaps in her memory perked Saori up. Akio could see the questions forming in her head as she found a few pieces of the same puzzle Akio so feverishly worked to complete. "Genjiro! I remember."

Heart racing, Akio leaned in.

"It was early on, but there was someone maybe fifty or so. He had been on the *Taihō* for almost as long as Baa-chan, but I can't be certain. I did see Ryū-ō. He was both frightening and beautiful. His aura encircled Genjiro and I felt a tingling. I haven't thought of that moment since."

"He must have erased your memory," Akio exclaimed. Another piece was falling in place.

"But why?"

"Why?" Akio hummed as he pondered. "Could the two be related?"

"What two?"

"Those who receive the gift and those who choose to give up."

Saori fell deep into thought. Akio tried to follow that trail, but he faltered. The confidence he'd had moments before evaporated, leaving him scrambling to hold onto the tiny thread he'd begun to unravel. It took several long seconds before he accepted defeat and acknowledged that his attempts were futile. He'd been so close. He was so certain. As Akio reached his conclusion, he saw Saori look up in defeat. The answer proved to be too elusive.

"We've never had more than thirty people aboard," Saori began.

Akio waited for her to finish her thought. Her words came out slowly, each one weighted as she carefully formed her thoughts.

"I need to talk to Yamada-sama," she announced abruptly. The moment of understanding had been broken for both of them. "There must be things she knows that she can tell me. Give me a few days and I will have more. She's acting in Senchou's stead so I may need more time."

The two ended their conversation determined to figure out what was going on. Saori seemed to be in higher spirits, a noticeable spring to her step as she went about her morning. For his part, Akio took note of his elevated spirits. He needed to keep an eye on Taka, but he was certain that he was on the right track. It was time to enjoy his time on the *Taihō*, as long as he didn't lose himself to her mysterious powers.

IX

Days passed and Akio found himself adjusting to life on the *Taihō* quite nicely. The warm sun and soft sea breezes left him wanting to find an empty spot on the ship so he could nap. The salty sea air left him refreshed every night just before bed. His afternoons kept him busy, however. As the newest member of the group, Akio spent countless hours with Taka and the others practicing their new songs. By the end of every session, Akio's hands ached. He longed for the day when the bachi would no longer irritate his hands, when the blisters would stop.

During this time, there was no sign of the captain. Mizuki ran the ship just as smoothly as Toshio did, navigating the sea as if it were second nature. To his relief, no one forgot about the captain like they did Satō. Conversations about him resting in the Captain's Quarters and speculation about his recovery occurred almost daily. For that, Akio was relieved.

As he did every other day, Akio stretched, ensuring his body was loose and limber to practice. The sun beat down on him as he lay shirtless on the deck, his left leg and torso twisting as he stretched. It had been a while since he last spoke to Saori and he wondered if he should reach out to her. His quiet contemplations were interrupted by the booming *don* of the ōdaiko.

Sitting up, Akio saw Mizuki striking the large drum. There didn't appear to be any approaching ships. A meeting. Slipping on his shirt, Akio made his way to the crowd forming at the helm. Spying Taka and the others up front, Akio decided to stay towards the back. He didn't like the thought of being surrounded for some reason. The thunderous beats continued for a little longer before Mizuki put down her bachi.

Facing the crew of the *Taihō*, Mizuki addressed the crowd with her mousy voice. "Good afternoon!" Her voice rang out despite its high pitch. "I come with good news. Our dear captain has informed me that he is feeling stronger. With the help of Ryū-ō, let us hope he will resume his post soon."

This was met with a resounding cheer from everyone on board. Akio's spirits flared. He'd always liked the grandfatherly man, and knowing he was steadily on the mend bought him great joy.

"Please," Mizuki said, raising her hands to quiet the crew. "That is not all. Senchou has also informed me that we will be pulling into shore to pick up a new crew member." Akio's heart dropped. Though he knew what this meant, he wanted to see how the process worked. "Let's make sure to welcome our new member and bring them into our family." Bowing to the crew, Mizuki said, "Let's have a good day."

The crowd in front of her bowed in return, a resounding "let's have a good day" filling the air. As the group dispersed, Akio scanned the deck. Taka and the others went down, probably to bring up the drums. Akio decided that he would not join them for practice and went to find a quiet spot to collect his thoughts.

He should have expected it at some point. Since Satō's departure, there had only been twenty-nine aboard. Saori said their number never exceeded thirty. If the *Taihō* brought him aboard as some chosen being, it would eventually welcome new souls after. The question became did they have a hand in their own demise? Akio had a sinking feeling that there was a good chance they did. Leaning against the side of the ship, Akio closed his eyes with a sigh. How many people had the *Taihō* carried over the centuries? The thought of countless spirits sailing for eternity because they believed the darkness was the better alternative left Akio's heart aching.

Memories with Miyako kept Akio floated between his musings. Now that he could see her face, the pain of what he inflicted upon her somehow hurt more. He'd dreamt about his last moments several times since his conversation with Satō, but the ones with his sister were more frequent. They were happy memories – small snippets of their childhood to remind him of the good times, and that brought a smile to his face. Peace washed over him, masking the sadness.

"I wonder if Inoue still gets good memories?" Akio wondered out loud, his eyes still closed. Snapping his eyes open, Akio was struck with a thought. "Did Satō-san stop having them? Did he lose the good times?"

The look of acceptance on Satō's face the last time they spoke flashed in his mind. There was a finality in his eyes, as though he lost all hope. And he'd been okay with that. Pushing himself up, Akio made his way towards the heart of the ship. He needed to find Saori. He wanted to discuss his ideas.

ত৵৹

It took a while before Akio managed to find Saori grabbing a snack from the pantry. He wanted to pull her from the others, but he didn't want to draw and attention, though it probably wouldn't make a difference. So he waited. Saori and the others shared their ideas about who Mizuki would take to pick up the new person and who would be left in charge.

Akio's ears perked up at the conversation, wondering if Saori brought up the topic on purpose.

"How often do either Yamada-sama or Senchou – or does he never leave – go to shore to pick up new crew?" Akio asked.

"I don't remember anyone other than you," one of the women in the room answered.

Akio believed her name was Chiyo, and her aura was motherly. She and Mizuki were almost like the crew's mothers.

"It's been a while and, to be fair, the days all blend together," Chiyo added. "But I remember that it's always Yamada-sama who goes while Senchou remains on board. I remember when she brought me on. She was so sweet. I was terrified because I'd never been on the water before."

"Me neither," the other woman said. "Yamada-sama does a wonderful job making us feel safe."

"I saw Yamada-sama speaking to Oda-san," Saori cut in.

Akio noted her use of honorifics around the ladies. Maybe she was only informal around him. The idea brought a smile to his lips.

"Maybe the two of them will head out soon," Saori suggested.

"Do we have a smaller boat or does the *Taihō* go?" Akio asked.

Confused mumbling and curious glances were exchanged. Akio noticed that Saori observed the others as well. The two made eye contact and Saori moved to excuse herself. Sharing a little small talk with the others, Akio waited a few minutes before he took his leave as well. He didn't have to go far before Saori pulled him aside.

"Did you catch that?" she asked. "No one really remembers more than their arrival."

"I noticed," Akio replied. "To be fair, I don't actually remember anyone coming with Yamada-sama."

"Me neither," Saori agreed. "But did you notice something?"

"No. What?"

"I thought that since we have space on the ship with Satō's departure, that this new arrival was linked. What if they aren't? There were thirty years between our arrivals."

Akio's brows knotted in confusion. Rubbing his chin, he tried to recall everything he'd learned in the last week. Parts of it came easily to him, while others popped up for a brief moment, trickling away like water in a sieve.

"Is it possible someone left and you never noticed?" Akio asked.

"No," she replied. "I think I remember everyone. I mean, maybe someone slipped through the cracks and the ship worked its magic, but I feel like I would've remembered. And what about Baa-chan? No one came after her."

Akio frowned. That was a good point. If he and Saori were the newest arrivals in thirty years that had to be important. There's no way there's a thirty year gap with no deaths.

"Could the *Taihō* be judging us?" Akio asked. "We're chosen to pursue Ryū-ō, maybe the ship vets us before we even board, to make sure we're suited for the task."

"Or gift," Saori said. "Bad people wouldn't just be put on a magical ship to play music, drink, and hunt for a god for eternity. That alone could be a blessing. No, I think you're on to something."

"Exactly," Akio said, excitement taking over. "Maybe I took Baa-chan's place and this new person is taking Satō-san's."

"Yes! There's never been more than thirty people on the *Taihō* at a time."

"Okay, so we have a cursed ship that erases our memories, gives us eternal adventure, and maintains a steady number of passengers. Could this be the god's ship?"

"Possibly. But wait," Saori's brow furrowed. "There's the Kingr and Zhōnghuá. I've never thought about it before, but if we're a ghost ship, how would they see us? How can our attacks hurt them?"

Akio hummed, pondering the implication of that statement. The Kingr didn't seem like much of a threat, despite them being alive. The drums' soundwaves or whatever it was beat them handily. The Zhōnghuá, however, were a mystery.

"This might be a question for Yamada-sama," Saori said. "She's spent more time with both of them. Maybe she'll have more insight."

The two spent the rest of the day walking around the perimeter of the ship. Taka and Watanabe – he'd really have to find time to remember the man's name – called out to him a few times inviting him to join in their practice, but Akio declined. His hands were sore from the blisters and he just wanted a break. It was too beautiful out to slave away at the drums for hours. Akio hadn't taken a day to relax in a long time. Even when he was alive, his life was spent inside a drab, yellow-walled building typing away on his computer. Each keystroke was a countdown to his death, and the constant clickity-clack brought him more and more dread.

Now, he felt alive, at peace. The sun warmed his flesh, invigorating him. The salty tang of the sea air cleared his lungs, pushing away all the dark thoughts that plagued him. His memories of the past, all of his self-loathing of not being good enough were exhaled away and floated off on the breeze. For the first time in a long time, Akio found himself smiling. His soul felt rejuvenated.

All the while, Saori mirrored him. Akio observed her creep out of her shell, a playful twinkle sparkling in her eye and a mischievous grin tugging on her lips. Her life had been normal, just like his. As she delved more into her past, Akio found some threads in her life that were strikingly similar to his. As they progressed, a shadow passed over her and she tucked a strand of hair behind her ear. She was only sixteen. Before she could move on, Akio grabbed her hand, stopping the conversation and redirect their train of thought to something more light-hearted. Now was not the time for death. There was more than enough surrounding them.

As the sun began to set, a crowd formed on the starboard side. A few people played the ōkedō as they spoke to someone nearby. Rounding the corner, Akio saw Mizuki and Oda climbing into a small rowboat. The two made their way over to join in with the others and their well wishes. As the boat was lowered into the choppy sea, Akio watched as the solitary lantern bobbed on the waves. He wondered if that would be enough to see by in the darkness when night had fallen.

Akio and Saori continued their walk late into the night. The sky was perfectly clear, a myriad of stars dotting the inky blackness of the heavens while the full moon shone brightly on the deck, hanging in the air like a giant pearl. A chilly breeze picked up the sails, flapping as they filled, before the two decided it was time to head in. Everybody was already asleep, light snoring greeting them as they entered the room. Locating a small space in the corner, Akio and Saori prepared for bed.

For the first time, Akio noticed that Saori curled up into a ball under her blanket. Sitting up, he scooted a little closer and began stroking her hair. Her body relaxed and she let out a small sigh before drifting off to sleep. However, Akio remained awake, watching Saori as she slept. Something within him stirred. Akio couldn't let Saori end up like Satō. He couldn't bear to watch her suffer like that. She'd managed to wiggle into his heart and he vowed to protect her.

X

ORNING CAME once again, this time to the agitated rocking of an angry sea. Akio was no longer alone when he woke. Ever since the newest member joined the crew roughly two weeks ago, Akio became the second-to-last to wake up. Rubbing the sleep out of his eyes, he groggily wondered if there was some magical hierarchy to waking up on the ship. Some kind of rule for seniority perhaps. Ever since the battle with the Kingr, he'd been noticing little quirks with life on the ship that he'd never picked up on before. Logging it away in the back of his mind, Akio added it to the ever-growing list of questions he had.

Making sure to not wake the new guy, a man in his sixties named Tanaka Daisuke, Akio went to grab his breakfast before starting his new chores. Mizuki made the same speech that Toshio had when Akio first joined the crew and right before their hunt for Ryū-ō. The more he thought about it, Akio became certain that they just repeated their message over and over as no one appeared to recognize it was the same every time. His suspicions grew as he thought about how both Toshio and Mizuki mentioned that they didn't know how the great dragon chose who was blessed. Saori said they both knew the truth about the *Taihō*. Surely, they knew the truth about the god's gift.

Standing in line for his miso, Taka called out to him, waving Akio over. The hot soup warmed Akio nicely as he sipped his breakfast. Taka and the usual group sat together finishing their meal. A rousing chorus greeted Akio as he approached.

"Enjoying not being the new guy?" Watanabe jibed. "I remember those days."

The group broke out into conversation reminiscing about their time on the ship. Akio blocked most of it out, although he did note how none of them seemed to realize they'd been on the *Taihō* for more than a few years. Three weeks passed since the Kingr attack, and all of the injured returned to their regular duties. Satō's absence had never been brought up after his departure. It was as if he never existed. Akio forced down his unease whenever this happened. Just like Satō, there wasn't any speculation or conversation about the captain. No one said a word. This also concerned him. And so, Akio continued his search.

All he could see were happy bodies enjoying a break from their morning duties as they ate. Tanaka already found a group of similarly aged people and they were laughing like old friends. A small flicker of envy flashed through Akio. Though he belonged to a clique, he was jealous that Tanaka fit in so seamlessly with no care in the world. As one of the younger crew members, Akio didn't have much in common with his peers. Finishing his daily search, Akio returned to his meal. No sign of the captain.

"Are you kidding me?" Taka's exclamation made the distracted Akio jump. "When did you see them?"

"Maybe a few hours ago, during first light. Three of them, including the damaged one."

"Damn Kingr!" Taka hissed. "Why can't they leave Ryū-ō alone? Don't they have their own gods?"

"What if they don't know he's a god?" Akio asked. A sudden sensation of floating filled him, muffling all other conversation. It reminded him of the tingling feeling he'd felt with Saori. In the background he heard Watanabe explaining something, but he wasn't listening. A surety like he'd never felt before hit him. "They don't know he's a god." Akio whispered his discovery into his miso while Watanabe droned on.

"Do you think we'll run into them today?" someone asked.

"Hard to tell," Watanabe replied. "If not today, soon."

"Let's start practice early today," Taka said. "We'll need to be in top form Katō. This will be your first battle, right?

Akio nodded, trepidation settling in his stomach like a rock. He didn't want to hurt anyone, but he also didn't want these hunters to hurt Ryū-ō. Images of the unfortunate Kingr who fell overboard during their last encounter flashed in his mind – the heavy wooden boats slamming together where his golden-haired head bobbed left Akio feeling weak.

His face must have paled because Taka clapped him on the back. "Don't worry. They've never boarded *Taihō*. We've got Ryū-ō's protection. You'll be fine."

Akio mumbled an incoherent response, taking a sip of his now-empty miso to distract him. Taka and the others resumed their conversation, leaving Akio to his thoughts. There had to be a way to avoid another confrontation with the Kingr. There's no reason anyone else should die. Could Akio even die if he didn't want to? What would happen if they did? Images of Satō floating serenely on the waves flashed in his mind. Akio abruptly stood up, drawing questions of concern from his friends, but he didn't respond. Instead, he wandered off, dropping his bowl with one of the cooks before circling the perimeter of the ship.

Heavy clouds hung overhead, blocking the sun and painting the skies a gradient of blacks and greys. White salt spray crested the sides of the ship, the *Taihō* rocking roughly in the angry waves. The mood reflected the turmoil swirling inside Akio. Emotions roiling between confusion to fear mimicked the mighty swells, with no ray of hope to be found. Still he paced. The winds picked up, pulling on Akio's clothes, whipping his hair, and shoving his body into the side of the ship multiple times.

A dark bruise began to appear on his arm after a particularly vicious wave slammed Akio into the side, nearly tossing him overboard into the deadly waters below. Akio's stomach clenched at the violent motions and he ended up emptying it into the sea. His head swam as he attempted to regain his composure. Wiping his mouth with the back of his hand, Akio straightened up. His heart immediately fell.

A raven flag.

Panic swirled inside Akio, preventing him from thinking clearly. His head swiveled as he searched for someone to tell. He wanted to shout a warning, but his mouth was dry and his stomach threatened to revolt again.

"Kingr... Someone... boat!" Akio's cry came out as a disjointed mumble, his voice lost on the winds.

A second flag came into view. Then a third. They were ready for war. Shoving himself from the edge of the ship, Akio stumbled as the ever-angry waves nearly toppled him, dropping Akio to his knee. Why was no one around? He struggled to the helm, clinging to anything he could to keep him upright. Everyone was gone. The rough waters must have pushed them below deck. Rain began to fall, pelting the deck. It wasn't long before Akio stood soaked, his clothes clinging to his body. The winds howled, chilling Akio to the bone as he tried to find someone.

Finally, he heard a shout from above. Craning his neck, he saw two figures in the crow's nest waving to him. Their cries were ripped from their throats and carried on the wind.

"I can't hear you!" Akio shouted, his hands cupped around his mouth.

Leaning over the edge of the nest, the man copied the movement and yelled: "Go inside!"

"Kingr!" Akio cried over and over as he pointed towards the incoming ships. He waved his arms wildly to accentuate his point.

The first man followed Akio's movements. Through the rain, Akio tried to make out what they were doing. At last, the first man hit his partner in an excited manner and the two began descending from the crow's nest. Exhaustion flowed through Akio, making his legs wobble.

"Go you idiot!" one of the men called out as he raced past Akio. "Get inside."

"But," Akio stuttered.

Both men already disappeared into the heart of the *Taihō*, a trail of water slicking the smooth wooden floors and creating small puddles where their feet fell. With a surge of adrenaline, Akio followed the pair into the shelter of the ship's walls.

Inside the ship, an eerie sense of foreboding hung in the air. Despite the men shouting in the distance, the stillness and quiet from the storm left Akio feeling as though time had stopped. Even the rocking of the ship felt muted. His vision struggled to adjust to the bubble he walked into. A figure rushed towards him, two more in pursuit. He tried to speak, but his voice caught in his throat. Without acknowledging him, Mizuki and the watch crew sped past him towards the helm. His body followed numbly, his feet taking him back above deck.

The trio assume their positions, Mizuki at the helm and the two scaling the mast to resume their post to keep an eye on the approaching ships. It was as though he were in a trance, his body moving on its own. The bubble returned, swallowing him up. A sudden tug on his arm snapped Akio from his stupor.

"Get in here," Saori hissed as she yanked him below deck once more and towards the sleeping quarters. "It's going to get rough."

"What's going on?"

"We're running. It's too dangerous to fight like this."

Saori led Akio to the sleeping quarters. The rest of the crew sat huddled together, waiting quietly as the waves tossed the ship side to side. Akio and Saori found a space and took a seat as a particularly rough wave threw them into Watanabe. The wind howled through the halls, now filling the rooms with its ominous cry. Water dripped off Akio, a puddle forming beneath him as it trickled down his body. Wiping his face with a soaked hand, Akio sat in shock. Soft chatter broke out after time passed.

"Are you okay?" Saori whispered. She leaned into him, concern etched on her face. "You seem out of it."

Akio nodded, disoriented. He felt out of it. It reminded him of the moment when he decided to go to his high school and jump. Everything moved with a robotic efficiency, all emotion and thought overridden by his body. Akio could see Saori and her fear, but his body would not react.

"What happened?" she asked, lightly touching his arm.

"I- I don't know," he muttered. "I just had a moment where I panicked. I don't want to kill anyone. I don't like how I felt before I died. I can't kill."

"It's okay," Saori soothed, pulling him into a hug. "You're okay."

Akio allowed himself to be held by her, his body in shock from the overwhelming surge of emotions, as she made soft shushing noises. The volatile waves died down, the winds following suit after a while. All that remained was the sound of rain hitting the deck. As the waves calmed, a similar tranquility engulfed Akio as he leaned into Saori's shoulder. The shock faded until it became a tiny flicker buried under other emotions - primarily relief as no calls for crew to rush above deck for battle were heard.

The savory aroma of seasoned fish and pickled vegetables heralded dinner. Akio never noticed anyone sneak off to prepare food, but his grumbling stomach was grateful they thought to do so. Bowls trickled into the sleeping quarters as the food was served to the crew, and Akio took his with a word of thanks. Everyone ate in relative silence; any conversation heard was soft and fleeting.

As people began settling down for bed, Mizuki and the two from the crow's nest finally walked into the sleeping quarters. Akio and the others perked up, curiosity and tension filling the room. Mizuki looked haggard, her body sagging as water ran down in rivulets. Her lips were blue, a stark contrast to her pale face and hands, and her teeth chattered despite her attempts to control them. Behind her, the two from the crow's nest stood shivering as they sloughed off their sopping clothes. Chiyo and Oda rushed over to the three with blankets and hot bowls of soup.

"Is everything okay, Yamada-sama?" Chiyo asked as she tried to dry Mizuki off. "What about the Kingr?"

Murmuring her thanks to the woman, Mizuki took a moment to drink some soup to warm up. Color returned to her face and fingers and her lips returned to their natural color, her teeth no longer chattering.

"We managed to evade them for now," Mizuki said. "But that probably won't last for long. Let's all be on alert. There are three ships pursuing us, and they will catch us. Be sure of that. However, we will be ready. Lights out. We need our energy."

Bodies jumped into motion as people prepared for bed. More blankets were passed to Mizuki and the two lookouts before the trio walked out to dry off. Exhaustion washed over Akio once more and his eyes suddenly felt very heavy. Searching for a pillow, Akio curled up under a blanket. A warmth spread over his back. Saori pressed against him, curled like a cat as she slept. Grateful for the physical contact, Akio let sleep overtake him. The day had been long and all he needed was a chance to relax and recover.

XI

OR THE FIRST TIME since he joined the crew, Akio woke
up before anyone else. The moon still hung in the sky,
the stars twinkling in the heavens. The scent of fresh
rain filled him. He'd always loved those spring days just after
the rain. In the crow's nest, the night watch joked about, calling out to Akio as he wandered about the deck. Making a turn
towards the helm, Akio decided to ask Ichirō if there had
been any of the Kingr. Instead, he was greeted by their captain, Toshio.

"Senchou," Akio gasped. "How – I thought you were still
hurt."

Toshio stepped out from behind the wheel, a kind smile
illuminated by the moonlight. Bandages wrapped around the
captain's lean arms and Akio thought he saw the outline of
more bandages under his shirt. A chilly wind blew past, but
Toshio showed no sign of discomfort. A twinge of longing to

run and hug the elderly man almost overcame Akio as he gazed upon the man who reminded him of his grandfather. Even in the moonlight, the little fox sigil caught his eye.

"It comes and goes, but I'll survive," Toshio said. "How are you?"

A knowing expression crossed Toshio's face as Akio attempted to stammer out a response. Akio thought he saw something else as well. Pity? Sorrow? He couldn't quite put his finger on it, but it was definitely there.

"Walk with me," Toshio said, extending his arm when Akio still couldn't produce a response. "I think there's much we need to talk about."

It didn't take more prompting for Akio to hurry over to the captain's side. The two set off on a leisurely stroll around the perimeter of the ship. The pair retraced Akio's familiar steps that he'd taken many times since Satō's departure. Their journey passed in silence, and Akio wondered what Toshio had to say.

"Such a beautiful night," Toshio said with a sigh.

Looking up, Akio took in the heavens. Sparkling stars dotted the night like diamonds. By now, the sun was preparing to rise, so instead of the inky blackness, the sky boasted a purple-black that looked almost like rich velvet. Accenting it all was the silver moon illuminating the deck with her gentle glow. He hummed in agreement.

"There's always a serene beauty as things end."

The statement perked Akio up. It seemed a strange thing to say. Part of him wanted to remain quiet to hear what else the captain had to say.

"But there's beauty in new beginnings as well." Toshio pointed to the horizon where the faintest glimpse of sunrise could be seen."

"And loneliness," Akio replied.

Toshio stared at him with a puzzled expression. "How so?"

Akio paused. The thought had just come to him, but he wasn't sure why. Some part of him deep down couldn't appreciate the beauty like Toshio.

"It's like life," Akio said simply. "We're born alone, and we die alone. Everyone ends up just fading away."

The weight of his own words hit Akio like a ton of bricks. The isolation he'd felt in life, just a nameless cog spinning around with others, slammed into him. Sure, there had been others just like him, but they focused on their own little section of the machine, slowly cranking away until their gears wore down and they were replaced. Everyone was replaceable.

"But the beauty is never forgotten," Toshio said kindly. "There are countless songs, poems, pictures – all about this fleeting moment of transcendence. It is exquisite. Like life. Nothing is so fleeting that it fails to touch at least one person. There is the beauty. Just like life."

For some reason, Akio found himself unable to look at Toshio. It may have been the shame he felt imagining this conversation with his own grandfather. Maybe it was the bond he felt with the elderly man, as though the captain considered Akio one of his own. Or perhaps it was the pain he felt as he imagined the gaping void that must swirl around in his loved ones' lives. Something dark and empty that could never be filled. Everything hit Akio all at once, sending him reeling into a spiral of emotion.

"You should never feel ashamed," Toshio said, his voice cutting through the miasma of Akio's turmoil. "We all have moments where the weight of it all overwhelms us. Our decisions define us, and clearly you were given a second chance. The *Taihō* does not allow just anyone to board her. That alone is a blessing. There are no others like her to my knowledge."

"Then how can the Kingr see us?" Akio asked.

"I've never really understood it myself. My guess is that since we've been blessed with this physical body, we are able to interact with the living. There is still much I must learn as your captain."

A wave of longing and hope washed over Akio, stronger than anything he'd felt since boarding the Taihō. He tried tempering his emotions, not wanting to open himself to disappointment, but the possibility tugged at his very core.

"Can I see my family?" he whispered.

Toshio shook his head sadly. Akio could see his own disappointment mirrored in the captain's eyes. Heaving a sigh, Akio pushed down his emotion. He knew it had been a long shot.

"The *Taihō* has few rules, but they must be obeyed. We are bound to the ship for all eternity. The only way to leave is by giving up our second chance, or by Ryū-ō himself. Such are the gifts of the god."

Humming in acknowledgement, Akio turned his attention to the rising sun. Streaks of pink and orange intertwined with the inky purple of night, heralding the sun. There was a beauty in the sunrise, the explosion of vibrant colors banishing the darkness for another day. Resting his elbows against the side, Akio let himself get lost in the serenity of the morning. He may not have admired the night, but he wouldn't ignore this moment.

"It is beautiful," Akio murmured.

Leaning next to Akio, Toshio let out a sigh as he rested on the siding. "It is."

The two stood in silence as they admired the birth of a new day. The golden light of the sun-bathed Akio with an inner peace, washing away everything else.

"Harmony leads to transcendence," Toshio said. "The *Taihō* helps us find the beauty that we once forgot."

Akio spun to face the elderly man, his mouth opened in question, but Toshio ignored him. He stood next to Akio in silence, his arm lightly resting on Akio's shoulder and a faint smile on his lips as the sun reflected off of his fox mon. The two stood together long after the sun crested the horizon.

XII

"RAVEN FAST APPROACHING!" a voice called out from the crow's nest. "Three!"

Panicked steps thundered up to the deck as everyone down below rushed up. Taiko were carried up, their stands slipping under the drums in the chaos. Taka called out orders for everyone to remain calm as he struggled to correct the placement of the drums on the stands.

"Keep calm!" Taka ordered. "Fear will not aid us."

Akio and the captain moved between the crew, practically unnoticed by the others. Using his good arm, Toshio straightened stands, managing small things for the others.

"Take your spot next to me," Toshio commanded Akio. "I cannot lead on my own."

Akio attempted to sputter out a response, but the captain raised his hand to silence him. Mizuki and Saori made their way to the ōdaiko. Upon seeing the pair, both women uttered gasps of surprise. Saori flung herself onto Akio while Mizuki rushed to the captain.

"I thought you left," Saori exclaimed, her eyes wide in terror.

"Senchou!" Mizuki gasped. "You should be resting."

Saori slapped Akio as he stared at her, perplexed. Next to them, Mizuki attempted to usher the captain back below deck.

"Why would you think that?" Akio asked, rubbing his arm where she smacked him.

"You were so out of it," Saori explained.

Mizuki continued to fuss over the captain. Hustling bodies rushed past them, their figures little more than a blur.

"Enough!" Toshio snapped at Mizuki. "Please let me manage myself."

"But Senchou," Mizuki begged. "Your arm."

"I can manage just fine," Toshio repeated firmly.

Saori waited for Akio, her eyes boring into him expectantly. Unsure of how to respond, he focused on the captain and Mizuki. The two moved away to share a word in private, forcing Akio to address Saori. He pulled her in, his arms wrapping around her slim frame.

"I wouldn't leave you like that. I promise."

Tears brimmed in the corners of Saori's eyes and she attempted to blink them away. Bodies bumped into the two of them without so much as an apology.

"Katō!" Taka's voice rang over the chaos. "We need you. Get over here."

"Kingr fast approaching!" the crow's nest called out.

Meeting Saori's gaze, Akio gave her a kiss on the forehead.

"I promise," he insisted. Turning to Taka, Akio called out, "I'm watching Senchou."

The rushing on the deck slowed as heads searched for their leader. Soft exclamations broke out as they spied the captain for the first time in almost a month. Noticing the attention was on Toshio, Akio craned his neck to see what happened next. Toshio faced the crew of the *Taihō*, standing tall despite the injuries to his body. At his side, Mizuki still moved to help him, stopping short so not to displease the elderly man. Hobbling to the helm, Toshio scanned the crowd, his gaze landing on Akio.

"It brings me great joy to see you all working so diligently to keep the *Taihō* and all aboard safe. I'm sure my absence has been difficult, so I thank you for everything you've accomplished."

The lone clapping from Toshio rang over the silence. Akio noticed the blood flowing to his face as he flushed. He didn't feel like he did anything worth the captain's adulation. Others must have shared Akio's embarrassment as they shifted from foot-to-foot.

"We don't have much time," Toshio continued as the echoes of his applause faded away. "The Kingr are fast approaching. Let's work together to chase them away once more. We are blessed by Ryū-ō. Let's thank him for his generosity. We are *Taihō*!"

Pumping his fist into the air, Toshio was greeted with the resounding chant of "We are *Taihō*!" by the crew. Each round of the chant grew in strength. At its peak, Akio's voice cracked, now scratchy from the vigor of his cheer. The cries continued for several long minutes before dying down. In the distance, singing from the Kingr returned the *Taihō*'s cry.

It was as if a light turned on. The crew of the *Taihō* resumed the preparations with the smooth efficiency they had the first time Akio joined them for battle. No longer did they scramble around, their actions frantic and sloppy. With Toshio back at the helm, Mizuki and Saori took their positions at the ōdaiko, its resounding booms invigorating the crew. Akio stood by the captain, his hands twitching from nerves as he shuffled his feet.

A sword was pressed into his hand by a passerby as they went to their post. Akio spied Daisuke, the man standing awkwardly as he alternated between watching the Kingr approach and wanting to help. Akio didn't envy the man.

"Are you ready?" Toshio asked, startling Akio.

"Yes sir," he stammered back.

"I'll need you to help me steer," Toshio explained. "I can't turn the wheel myself."

Humming in response, Akio froze as his blood ran cold. Though they were still a distance away, he heard the haunting song. The Kingr sang for their god. The rich vibrant tones of their voices harmonizing between the three ships still mesmerized him.

"Don't let them scare you," Toshio soothed. "The Kingr are fierce warriors and if we stand any chance, we must hold strong."

With a gulp, Akio nodded. The song sounded like death speeding towards him. He remembered how viciously the Kingr fought last time. He had no purpose then. Now, Akio knew his part. He would protect the captain, and by extension his family on the *Taihō*. Placing his sword on the ground, Akio braced himself.

"Yes sir," Akio murmured. It wouldn't be easy though.

As if Toshio read his mind, the captain said in a grandfatherly tone, "It takes a while to push the power of their song away. You're not the first to fall prey to it. I remember my first time hearing it. I -"

The captain's words were cut short as a hail of arrows rained down on the Taihō, their number darkening the sky. Rushing to the helm, Akio helped Toshio yank the wheel hard to the right. Voices cried out at the unanticipated attack, the drums sliding across the deck at the sudden movement. Akio grunted as his muscles strained against the wheel. His teeth gnashed together as his knuckles turned white. Saori and Mizuki yelped as they stumbled into the siding at the helm that protected the ōdaiko. As the booming of the taiko came to a sudden halt, the Kingr's chant reverberated in the air.

"Regroup!" Toshio called out.

Mizuki and Saori rushed back to the ōdaiko, resuming their beats. Taka and the others repositioned their drums, the shime tapping out a fast backbeat. The galloping pace stumbled in the beginning as they attempted to regain their composure. Akio noticed that even Taka appeared flustered, his strikes not having their usual intensity and sounding weak.

As the ship completed its turn, the sound of arrows slamming into the wood as they embedded themselves into the *Taihō* cut through the beating of the drums. No screams of agony rang out, giving Akio hope that no one was hurt. Releasing the wheel, Akio saw his fingers retained their gripped position, the muscles having seized from their efforts. Akio knew he needed to get back to the wheel quickly, so he shook his hands hoping to get the blood flowing back into his fingers. It took several agonizingly long seconds before his hands relaxed. In the background, the taiko players found their rhythm, and a familiar song rumbled in the air. The Kingr's song melded into the music of the taiko until the two became intertwined.

The anxiety that swirled inside Akio stilled as the taiko's power calmed him. Glancing to his right, the black of the raven flapped close to the *Taihō*. Akio marveled at how such a simple image could have such an impact on him.

Then the Kingr stopped singing.

A thunderous roar from the three Kingr ships rang out from over the boom of the ōdaiko. One ship pulled up next to the *Taihō*. Akio gazed in horror as the broken bust of the familiar ship pulled alongside them. The two ships that sailed with it split off, moving to flank the *Taihō*.

"Senchou!" Akio cried out, his voice panicked. "What do we do?"

A loud noise, like rushing water, sounded from the starboard side as the power of the taiko sped towards the longships. The blasts zoomed past the ships, clipping the backside of one and sending it reeling. Men toppled over the edge, some dangling over the side, as others splashed into the choppy waters. The longships still positioned themselves around the *Taihō*, ignoring their flailing brethren.

"We need to maneuver around them," Toshio said. "We can't let them box us in."

Straining on the wheel, Akio took hold, his hands next to the captain's. The *Taihō* began to list away from the longships as another hail of arrows sped towards the fleeing ship. A rising crescendo from Saori and Mizuki sent a blast of energy at the arrows, snapping them in half, causing them to plummet toward the sea.

"We're doing it!" Akio exclaimed as the *Taihō* put distance between herself and the flanking longships.

A moment later, a shuddering blow shook the ship as the damaged Kingr longship struck the *Taihō*'s side. As the *Taihō* rocked, the music stopped. Furious war cries rang out as a swarm of Kingr rushed to board the *Taihō* amidst another hail of arrows. Drums nearly toppled as men moved to both avoid the arrows and stop the Kingr's assault. Those with swords ran to chop the ropes connecting the two ships while Mizuki and Saori continued to play. Akio gasped as an arrow nearly found a home in Taka's flesh, his friend jumping out of the way at the last minute.

Daisuke puttered about, terrified and unable to do anything in the chaos. Releasing the wheel to a cry of protest from Toshio, Akio raced towards Daisuke. The golden head of a Kingr crested the *Taihō*'s side next to Daisuke, a wicked gleam on the warrior's face. In an instant, the attacker was on the ship. Several more quickly followed. Shouts of surprise and confusion rang out as the steel of sword met axe and hammer.

One of the Kingr raised his arm to strike Daisuke with his warhammer. As the head swung down, Akio managed to yank the bewildered Daisuke back, the older man toppling onto Akio as they landed together on the deck in a tangle of limbs. Daisuke stuttered out his thanks, his body frozen atop of Akio.

"Move!" Akio commanded. "Go to the sleeping quarters and hide."

Daisuke tried to object, but Akio shoved him off with a forceful command. A moment later, the head of the Kingr's hammer came at Akio's head. Rolling to his left, Akio felt the rush of air as the hammer struck the deck. Daisuke scuttled away as Akio jumped to his feet. He was still unarmed and not trained for combat. Regretting his decision to learn piano instead of kenpō, Akio faced the advancing Kingr alone.

The golden-haired warrior said something to Akio, flashing his teeth as he approached menacingly. The man's face was smeared with blue paint, three lines going down from forehead to cheek as though he were scarred. His hammer played in his hand, the man's fingers toying with the grip.

Then he attacked. Akio dodged out of the way as the man swung, leaping for the nearest patch of open space and crashing onto the deck. A loud splintering and gruff shout caused Akio to spin around instead of run. The hammer was embedded in the deck and the Kingr struggled to pull it free. Seizing his moment, Akio darted to the side of the ship.

His fingers fumbled with the hooks attached to the side. After a frantic struggle, Akio managed to pry them off, sending them and the accompanying Kingr into the sea. A sudden jolt nearly sent him over the edge as Toshio and Saori cranked the ship's wheel to create space between the *Taihō* and the other two ships.

A thunderous roar and the whooshing of air by his head startled Akio. He thanked Ryū-ō for the captain to have swerved at just that moment, throwing him off-balance. A yelp escaped his lips as the warhammer slammed into the side of the ship. Spinning around, Akio kicked the man on the thigh, hurting his toe in the process. The Kingr cursed as his leg buckled, giving Akio time to stumble back.

Akio knew he should run, but he couldn't take his eyes off the Kingr. His luck was running out and he feared the next strike would hit. Fast approaching feet from behind forced Akio to finally tear his gaze off his attacker. A second Kingr with an axe charged him. Akio's heart raced as he dropped to the ground to avoid the blade as it sliced through the air. The first Kingr came at him as well.

"Two?" Akio sputtered before his back hit the side.

His hands gripped the side of the *Taihō* as the two Kingr advanced. A terrified rhythm played in his chest as his heart slammed into his ribs. The pair bore down on Akio. His life began to flash before his eyes. Images of his parents, grandparents, and Miyako blinked before him. His first kiss with Yumi under the cherry blossoms. And Saori. They all went by in a blur.

The Kingr prepared to strike. Akio knew he was dead. With a deep breath, he accepted the end. As axe and hammer rushed towards him, Akio hoped that it would at least be painless. Relatively painless.

Then the ship lurched once more.

XIII

AIR HOWLED in Akio's ears as he plummeted to the chaotic waters below. He must have been the luckiest man on earth. When the *Taihō* turned, he fell over the side, the Kingr's attack missing him. Now he just needed to avoid getting crushed by the ships. The cold water hit Akio like a brick. His body smacked the sea, his limbs going numb and his back aching as it absorbed the blow, knocking the wind out of him. A moment later, he was enveloped by the waves.

The chill seeped into Akio's bones. His lungs burned as he struggled for breath. Akio's head broke the water and he gasped for air. He barely got a lungful before waves washed over him once more. The current pulled Akio back under, tossing him like a ragdoll. Akio fought to swim to the surface, but he was yanked underneath.

Wind hit him as he broke the surface once more, gasping for air. His clothes weighed him down and the waves pushed on him. Back on the ship, Akio could hear the chaos of battle, voices crying out, before he was shoved underwater once more. A particularly strong current pulled him away from the fighting and out into the open sea. By this point, Akio was exhausted. His limbs felt like lead weights dragging him down. The ships were getting further away, making it difficult for him to be noticed for rescue.

This was the end, Akio told himself. He would disappear in the ocean like Satō. Like Baa-chan. Like the countless others who came before him and probably would come after. He wasn't scared. He was much too tired to worry. All he hoped for was it to be quick and painless.

A wave rolled over Akio, and he began to sink. The sea wasn't as cold by this point. As the surface disappeared, Akio noticed that the water below him glowed. Drowning wasn't so bad after all. The bright light soon enveloped Akio, bathing him in an ethereal glow. A steady stream of bubbles surrounded him as they rose from the depths. Akio tried to kick, but found his legs moved slowly as if he were trapped in molasses. More bubbles appeared, followed by a blinding light.

A magnificent dragon swam up from the depths, its body undulating in the now-still waters.

Ryū-ō.

Akio, the god spoke in Akio's mind. His words rang powerful and clear. *You have shown yourself to be kind and brave, even in the face of peril. For your actions, I would like to reward you with my blessing.*

Akio's jaw dropped. He quickly closed it for fear of getting seawater in his mouth, but found he no longer needed to breathe. He wondered what the gift could possibly be.

My child, Ryū-ō said. *I offer you a second chance. To return to your old life as though nothing happened.*

The weight of the god's words sank in. He could go home. He could see his family. Yumi. He could see Miyako again. It was truly a wonderful gift. He then thought of Saori. He couldn't just leave her here, to suffer until she gave up. She'd struggled much too long by herself.

You hesitate, Ryū-ō noted, cocking his scaly head as if he were confused. *Is it because of the girl?*

Akio nodded. A stream of bubbles shot up towards the surface from the movement. He wasn't sure how best to communicate, but it appeared the dragon could see his desires.

Your sister mourns your loss every day, Ryū-ō explained. *I can see your heart. You want nothing more than to embrace her. More than your own mate. Are you sure that's what you want?*

The question felt ominous. Treading the water despite the glow keeping him suspended in the water, Akio played with his options. It was so easy. Why did he even doubt himself? Akio didn't take long to solidify his decision in his heart. Miyako's face burned in his mind. He could hear her soft voice echoing in his mind.

"Welcome home, Onii-chan!"

He felt her arms wrap around his body, squeezing him like only she could. It was time to go home.

❧

The sun beat upon Akio's back. The sky was a clear cobalt blue, and not a cloud marred its perfection. People called out to him, wishing him a good morning as he walked by. Finding a small bit of shade, Akio wiped the sweat from his brow. The salty tang of the sea air reinvigorated him. Toshio came up behind him, stopping at the wheel. It was nice seeing the elderly man up and about again. Months had passed since Akio encountered Ryū-ō. No one acknowledged his appearance, just like they never mentioned Saori's disappearance.

"You did a noble thing," Toshio had told him after Akio sought him out.

Toshio was right. Giving Saori a second chance saved her from a fate Akio knew would come if he'd accepted the gift for himself. As much as he missed his sister, he knew he would see her again. He just needed to wait for Ryū-ō to find him again. Fingering the mon that appeared on his shirt the day after his encounter with the mighty god, Akio smiled.

The vibrant threads of the fox gleamed in the sunlight. His grandfather had been right. Harmony leads to transcendence.

About the Author

K.N. NGUYEN is a fantasy author and founder of DragonScript. Growing up, she often found herself immersed in some imaginary world, conquering enemy nations, and saving the day. As time went on, her love for horrible puns and nerd culture pulled her out of these worlds and brought her back to reality.

It wasn't until she started working at her office job that she felt the itch to begin writing. Since 2015, she's been bringing her stories to life, one-by-one, and following her passion by delving into new mythologies.

A native of Sacramento, California, K.N. Nguyen spends her time singing karaoke, playing taiko, enjoying rhythm dancing games, and traveling with her friends and family when she isn't writing.

Other Works by K.N. Nguyen

King's Blood

Oath Blood

God's Blood

Nightmare Blood

Dragon Script

Lost Chapter

A Song of Strength